LIFE AIN'T FAIR

"BUT"

THE GAME IS COLD

SHAVONDA KING

B/B

BrianaB Publishing

GARY, INDIANA

This book is a work of fiction based on the author's imagination. The characters, names, and places are all fictionalized.

Visit my website at

www.brianab1.com

Cover design: www.garciat@hotmail.com

Cover Photograph: Tito G. / TotAlii Vision

Acknowledgements

First and for most, I would like to thank my Lord and Savior Jesus Christ for dying for all my sins. Thank you father for blessing me and allowing me to borrow your daughter Briana Brooks. Whom I claim as my own She is the most beautiful, amazing, smart, funny and talented kid any mother could dream of asking for. I thank you father for allowing me to take ownership over her while we're on earth, believing in me and trusting me with her life. I promise to nurture her until the death of me.

To my entire family I love each and every one of you dearly. Thanks for your continued support.

To my daughter's father: Brian Brooks thank you for being a friend to me and a father to our child.

To PeeWee: One of the first people to love me and teach me a lot. Thank you for being apart of my life for so many years. You have always protected me and made me feel safe in your presence. No matter the distance between us. I will always love you from the bottom of my heart.

To my friends I love each and every one of you like sisters. We all have some great memories that we will forever cherish.

To my God-kids I love each and every one of you unconditionally

To my Co-Workers: Zoe Benyoun, Diane Fossett, and De'Angelo Nelson. I have had some great moments with the three of you. It was nobody but God that brought all of us close. I love all of you.

All my extended family member I love you all deeply.

I would like to thank my make-up artist Danielle Carter for going above and beyond to keep my face looking phenomenal.

I would like to thank Tiffany Woods for my lovely hair style.

I would like to thank my stylist Nicole Harmon Matthews

Special thank you to Mita Vain from Vain Entertainment & Productions. You are my manager, my friend, and my sister. I love you past death. I have come a long way because of your advice, help and support. There's nothing in this world that I could trade you for. I have learned so much from watching you and talking to you.

Special thank you to Chicago's own Actor and Model Twon Cruz for assisting me on this project. I must say we brought nothing but sexiness to the cover together. I really appreciate you and working with you.

I can't close this out without acknowledging two of my favorite men and my Angels in heaven. My grandfather, Miller P. King. No matter what I know you are always watching over me. I miss and love you so much. I think about you so much but as long as I know you are resting peacefully then I'm at peace. Look after the rest of the family and close friends for us. I love you daddy!!!

Monta' Henry you will always hold a special place in my heart. I have learned so much from you and you was nothing but a gift from GOD to me. I miss you ever day and I love you so much. Give Dad and Gank a kiss for me.

Sincerely,
Shavonda King

My'an Mack

I would like to acknowledge a very special young lady by the name of My'an Mack. She is from my hometown and is battling Lymphoma Cancer at the age of 8. She is a beautiful and sweet young lady and I would like for everyone to keep her uplifted in Prayer.

Chapter 1

After seeing all the killings in the hood Talonda never wanted her boys to grow up victims of society. She always wanted the best for all her kids, but she had to work on herself first. She had personal issues going on in her life that she never dealt with. She always felt like that's why she was never good at choosing the right men to bring in her kids' lives. She always wanted to move her kids out of the hood but she never could get her money together to do that.

The block she lived on had shootouts, dope spots getting raided, and in sum cases she even seen people get killed. A lot of people Talonda knew as a child ended up getting on drugs. Sum of her friends from school fell victim to the drug game as well. The temptation of dating a drug dealer was at its all-time high. It seem like those were the only dudes to date now days.

She was into older men though. All she wanted to do was find herself a good man that was willing to help her raise her seven kids and love just her. She didn't realize her kids were feeling like victims already. They wanted to live like normal kids and have fun. They was never able to do things other kids could do. They couldn't go to parties, school dances or even get involved in outside activities. D.J. was an ordinary kid who wanted to have a normal life. He didn't have the best clothes and shoes, because his mom had six other kids by five different men. D.J. was the oldest of seven kids. None of their fathers were in any of their lives. The youngest three dad was around for quite some time until they decided to leave for other women. The oldest four didn't know their dads or anything about their families.

For the most part their mother Talonda worked as a Medical Assistant and took damn good care of them as much as she could as a single parent. The only problem Talonda had was, she needed a man at all times in her life to validate who she was as a woman. She was never good at choosing the right men. She started messing with this one cat named Dre. Dre was a tall man who stood about 6ft. tall, slender built and a clean shaved head. He had a very deep intimidating voice when he talked. He didn't work all he did was leach off D.J's mom Talonda. D.J. didn't care for him because he didn't do shit but drink and eat up their food, sleep or either hangout in the streets. Talonda didn't care what Dre did as long as he came back home to her. One day D.J. asked Dre why he had so many scars on his arm. Dre spatted back at D.J. "these are war wounds"; "you wouldn't know anything about that Lil' Chump". D.J. cut his eyes at Dre while whispering to himself "yeah ok".

While Talonda would be at work she would leave Dre at the crib to watch the kids. He felt like they wasn't his kids so he would leave them at home by themselves for D.J to look after them. Since he was the oldest of the seven kids. D.J. couldn't do what the average twelve year olds could do. He could never go outside and play with the other kids. He was too busy being a father figure to his siblings. D.J. decided to ask his mom when she came in from work. "Why we can't go over Moma Tanya's house anymore?" She responded "Why D.J."? (Moma Tanya is Talonda's mother, but everyone called her Moma Tanya). D.J. responded to his mom, "Because we could outside and play when we are over her house." Talonda turned to D.J. and said "Well your granny don't like and respect Dre, "so until she can accepts him being the person I love and respect him we not going over there til she does."

D.J was too young to understand what she meant by that. He walked off saying under his breath "All I want to do is be a real kid." Talonda yelled out to D.J. "What the fuck did you just say?" D.J kept walking and

2

yelled back "Nothing mom nothing!" Talonda yelled back at D.J "You better watch who the fuck you talking to before yo ass get slapped!" Talonda had never spoken to D.J. like that before. D.J. went into the other room with his siblings and watched TV to avoid his mom. Dre had been gone most of the day he never checked on kids or anything. D.J. didn't know how cook so all he could feed them was cereal and noodles, until his mom came home to cook for them. D.J. would sit in the room thinking of a way out. He didn't like living with his mom anymore she was starting to change. All of a sudden she was too tired to do anything for them.

She started calling off work, because she couldn't get out of bed. She was always sick and tired. The phone rang D.J. answered it was his moms boss Mr. Thomas. D.J. tried waking her up, all she did was moan roll over and went back to sleep. D.J told her boss she was asleep and wouldn't wake up to get the phone. Her boss was furious, he told D.J. to tell her she didn't have to come back to work anymore. D.J. knocked on his mother's door and told her what Mr. Thomas said and she replied "Okay" and stayed asleep. D.J. being an average kid he didn't think anything of it. He went on bout his business and watching his siblings. DJ didn't know what to do he was only twelve years old, and the youngest was seven months old. DJ would stare out the window looking at the other kids play. Til one day he got tired of sitting in the house. He got himself dressed; found his eleven-year-old brother Desmond some clothes. His nine year old sister Shelly some clothes, his eight year old sister Destiney clothes, his six year old brother Aseanti clothes, His three year old sister Kelley clothes, and seven month old brother Devin some clothes and make him some bottles.

He packed as much as he could in him and Desmond book bags. He packed what he could in the baby's diaper bag. He put Devin and in the stroller and they all left the house walking to their grandmother's house. Talonda was out of it she didn't know they were gone. While the kids were on their way walking to their grandmothers house they spotted Dre sitting at an abandoned building looking like he was in the daze. DJ was trying to talk to him, and he was looking as if he didn't know who in the hell they were. He didn't ask the kids were they were headed or anything. DJ tried talking to Dre for about five more minutes, but all Dre would do was nod his head and doze off. DJ told the kids "come on yall he don't care about us." "We not his kids anyways." All seven kids continued trucking on down the street, headed to their grandmother's house. The kids were about six blocks away from the crib, and their aunt Tracey sees them. She pulled over and called out DJ's name. DJ stopped because the voice sounded familiar to him. "Where are yall going?" Asked Aunt Tracey. DJ replied "To Moma Tanya's house." "Where is yo moma?" Asked Aunt Tracey. "She's at home in the bed, where she's been for the last three days." Replied DJ. Aunt Tracey was pissed off because the kids were out there walking by themselves. "Where in the hell is her so called man at?" Asked Aunt Tracey. DJ said "he over sitting by the candy store at an abandoned building drunk or something."

Aunt Tracey piled the kids into her SUV to take them back home. She rolled pass Dre stretched out sleep at the abandoned building. She just shook her head and mumbled to herself "no good ass mother fucker!" When they made it back to Talonda's house, she was still passed out in the bed. Tracey woke Talonda up yelling at her "Why the fuck is you sleep and these kids out here walking across town by themselves?" Talonda mumbled something, but Tracey couldn't make out what she had said. Tracey snatched the covers off Talonda yelling at her. "Get yo ass up and take care of your kids!" Talonda kept mumbling and swinging her hands at Tracey to get her to leave her alone. Tracey knew something wasn't right; she piled the kids back into her SUV and took them to her mother's house. Moma Tanya was so happy to see all her grandbabies, she started hugging and kissing them.

Tracy barged in behind them yelling "Moma you need to find out what's going on with your daughter!" "What do you mean Tracey?" Asked Moma Tanya. Tracey replied "she at home drunk or something." "She passed out sleep and I see the kids walking on their way walking to your house." Moma Tanya told Tracey "calm down before you wake up Daddy." "He went to dialysis today and now he's resting." Moma Tanya told Tracey she will talk to Talonda and see what's going on. Tracey looked at her mom with a pissed off look and told her "well you need to hurry up because I wanna know too." Mama Tanya tried calling Talonda but she didn't answer. She told Tracey to sit with the kids and her dad while she went over there. Moma Tanya proceeded to go over to Talonda's house. When moma Tanya walked in Talonda was in the bathroom over the toilet throwing up, with her body drippin in sweat. Moma Tanya asked Talonda, Are you okay?" She was too busy throwing up her guts, she couldn't answer. She would say she was cold in between throwing up, but that was it.

Moma Tanya called the ambulance for Talonda. When the ambulance arrived Talonda refused to go to the hospital. One of the technicians checked her vitals, she had a slight temp and her respirations were very fast. Her blood pressure was a little high, but not too much. While checking her vital signs they noticed bruises on Talonda. They asked Moma Tanya if Talonda was a drug user. Moma Tanys told them "NO!" "She never used drugs a day in her life." "She has seven kids to support, and a good job." They offended Moma Tanya when they asked her that. The technicians showed Moma Tanya the bruises, she told them "it's probably that no good nigga she's with abusing her". She knew one thing her daughter wasn't on no drugs. Talonda all of a sudden spazzed out on them. She started yelling and hollering for everybody to get the hell out her house. Not one time did she ask where her kids were? She didn't even realize they were gone.

The Emergency Technicians gathered their things and informed Moma Tanya that if Talonda refused their help its nothing they can do, because she's conscious and competent. Moma Tanya didn't want to hear that she wanted help for her daughter. She told them "look at her, you can clearly see she's sick." Once again they tried to explain it was nothing they could do if she refuse their help. Moma Tanya helped Talonda into the bathroom so she could clean herself up. She was too weak to bathe herself, so her moma helped her bathe. Moma Tanya helped her into her pajamas and back to bed. She fixed her a bowl of chicken noodle soup and crackers so she would have something on her stomach. Moma Tanya sat there a lil while longer to keep an eye on her. She decided to do a lil cleaning while Talonda rested. The only thing was running through Moma Tanya's head was, she hoped she wasn't pregnant again. Moma Tanya noticed Talonda didn't keep her house clean like she normally does.

She cleaned as much as she could without wearing her own self out. She still had to deal with the grandkids and Dad when she got back. After Talonda ate the soup she started to feel a lil bit better. Talonda called out and asked her mom "where are the kids?" "They were walking to my house and Tracey saw them." "She brought them back but you was so out of it, she just brought them to me." In the midst of their conversation Tracey called to tell her mother to bring the baby some more milk, because DJ brought what he could. Moma Tanya asked Talonda where was all the baby milk and cereal. Talonda said, "she hasn't gotten a chance to go to the store because she's been working a lot of hours." Moma Tanya just shook her head, grabbed the one can of formula that was there and left. Moma Tanya wanted to ask the kids what was going on so bad, but she didn't want to question them.

When she got back to the house, she had Tracey to take DJ to the store with her to get the baby some more formula, purified water and some cereal. Moma Tanya whispered to Tracey "ask DJ if he knew what was going on with his mom." Tracey said "I sure will because I would like to know also." Tracey and DJ went to the store. While they were in the car Aunt Tracey asked DJ "what is going on at home?" DJ replied, "What you mean Aunt Tracey?" "Have you noticed a change in yo mom?" Tracey asked DJ. DJ hunched up his shoulder and replied, "I don't know, all I know is, I want to be able to go out and play with other kids." Tracey asked DJ "why you all can't go outside?" DJ said, "Because I have to babysit while she's at work." Tracey frowned her face and said to DJ "I can't understand why you would be babysitting and she has childcare." "We don't go to anymore." Replied DJ

When they came to a red light, DJ was staring out the window at the kids playing and enjoying their summer vacation. He was looking at their nice shoes and clothes. His shoes and clothes were decent, but they weren't name brand like most of the kids his age. He and his siblings passed clothes down to one another. DJ was in a deep daze staring out the window that he blocked out him and Aunt Tracey's entire conversation. He was thinking real hard about what their lives would be like if they all had gear and toys to play with like the other kids on the block. Sometimes the kids would jive on them for wearing buddies, but it wasn't anything they could do. They couldn't call their fathers, because they didn't know them. Tracey noticed the blank stare on DJ's face as he was staring out the window. She just didn't know why. She didn't want to keep questioning him in case he shut totally down and don't want to talk anymore. DJ turned and looked at his Aunt Tracey and told her "one day imma make a lot of money, "and buy my brothers and sisters everything." Tracey jokingly said to DJ "well I hope you have a good job, because it's a lot of you lil motherfuckers running around here."

Tracey noticed DJ didn't find that too funny. She asked DJ what was wrong. "C'mon DJ talk to me." Replied Tracey. "She don't do none of the things she used to do." "She is always in the room with Dre or either sleeping." Replied DJ. Tracey responded, "well you know she's always working and she be tired." DJ cut his eye at Tracey and said very nonchalant "she use to work." Tracey replied "what u mean she use to work!" "Don't she still work?" DJ said, "she barely went to work this week and when her boss called to talk to her, "she wouldn't get up to get the phone." "So he said to tell her don't come back to work." "He sounded very upset on the phone." Tracey shook her head and said to herself "what the fuck is wrong with her?" DJ was in his own lil world thinking about how he could make money to support his family.

Dre wasn't doing shit to help them out, and now neither was his mom. The kids stayed at their grandmother's house for a couple days til their mom got herself together. Talonda decided to go into work, only to find out she had been fired. She begged and pleaded with her boss to keep her job, but he refused to keep her after doing two no call no shows. She was hysterical she didn't know what she was going to do. Her mom was calling her because the kids needed fresh clothes. So she went and picked the kids up. Her moma could see she was disturbed by something, but she decided not to say anything.

Tracey walked through the door with a loud tone "hey everybody!" everyone spoke except Talonda. Tracey asked Talonda very nonchalantly. "Why do you have on work clothes, didn't you get fired?" "STAY THE FUCK OUT MY BUSINESS!" Talonda replied to Tracey. Moma Tanya asked Tracey "what do you mean she got fired?" Moma Tracey uttered "Ta-Ta Talonda did you get fired?" Talonda responded with an attitude "yes mom I did!" Moma Tanya asked "why would they fire you and you were so dedicated to that job?" Talonda looked at her mom and spatted "I don't know mom and neither do I want to talk about it." "All I came to do was get my kids and go home." Talonda knew without a job it would be just a matter of time before everything start falling apart. Dre was missing in action.

DJ was getting so fed up with everything he wanted to run away from home, but he didn't want to leave his siblings behind. Dre came home a few hours later. DJ heard his mom and Dre arguing and fighting. DJ gathered all the kids took them into the back room and called his granny.

Meanwhile while Tracey & Moma Tanya was talking she told Tracey she thinks Dre beat on Talonda because of all the bruises on her. Tracey looked at her mom sideways and asked "what bruises moma?" Moma Tanya replied to Tracey "when the ambulance came to check Talonda out when she was sick, the paramedics asked if Talonda was a known drug user." Talonda was insulted by that. She told the paramedics she ain't never used a drug day in her life. "When I first saw the bruises on you that was the first thing to pop in my head." Said one of the paramedics. "If this ugly nigga put his hands on my baby, I would kill'em dead!" Said Moma Tonya. Tracey was in disbelief, but the both of them knew ever since Talonda got with Dre she changed a lot.

When Moma Tanya and Tracey arrived at the house the younger two children were crying from all the yelling and screaming that was going on. Dre had already left the house. Moma Tanya asked Talonda if she needed to take the kids with her. Talonda said "no mom everything is fine!" They knew Talonda didn't want to be bothered so they went on and left. DJ asked his mom if he could go outside, she told him yeah only if he took Desmond with him. DJ didn't care he just wanted to get out the. They would sit at home and dream about being rappers. They would write lyrics at home and rap them to each other around the crib. They knew it would take a lot of hard work and money to become a famous rapper. DJ would call himself DJ Money and Desmond would call himself D-Boy. They knew they didn't have the money to get the proper equipment they needed to make their beats.

It was a dream they always had but they didn't see it happening anytime soon for them. They didn't see anything happening anytime soon. They just wanted to live life to the fullest and take care of their family. The boys could finally go out to play, so they walked over to the court. They knew they weren't supposed to be over there, because the older dudes hung out over there.

Wherever DJ went Desmond was gonna follow. As the boys approached the court, Desmond asked DJ what that smell, "Weed!" was Replied DJ. "What's weed?" Asked Desmond. DJ shrugged his shoulders, "ugggh could you stop asking so many questions and just be happy we outside for once Desmond!" "Ok!" Replied Desmond.

A lil man a voice called out. Desmond looked up, and asked "who me"? "Naw!" "Not you the other lil dude." DJ looked up and replied "Who me?" The deep voiced dude responded "yeah you lil nigga." He looked at DJ and asked "aren't you the same lil nigga that be walking up and down the street with all them damn kids?" DJ responded, "yeah that would be me." DJ asked the deep voiced man. "Well since you know so much about me." "Then what's your name?" The deep voice replied, "I go by the name Dead Eye." Dead Eye pulled out a pocket full of money and gave DJ $20.00 and told him to buy him and his siblings some candy. DJ eyes lit up when he saw that knot in Dead Eyes hand. Dead Eye smirked and asked DJ why you looking like you never seen money before. DJ hunched his shoulders and said, "I don't know." "Maybe because I haven't." Dead Eye told DJ to come around sometime he would probably have some odd jobs for him to do to make a few dollars.

That was like having a job to DJ. DJ told Desmond "while I'm out working you will have to be the big brother for a while." Desmond looked up at Dead Eye and said "Mr. Dead Eye I wanna work too." Dead Eye told Desmond he might have a lil job for him as well. Desmond smiled and said "thank you Mr. Dead Eye". Dead Eye shook his head and said "leave the Mr. off, and just call me Dead Eye lil dude." Since their mom wasn't working this was a good way for them to make a lil money and take care of home.

Chapter 2

By the age of 13 this lil nigga DJ was ready to break bread. He was a straight go getta. He was gone do whatever he had to do to take care of home. He stood out on the block making a few hits here and there, for the older cats. He was more like an errand boy for them. He didn't care he just wanted to start stacking his loot. He started selling weed, so he can stack his own bread. He didn't want nobody to front him anything, because he didn't want to owe a motherfucker shit. He started making $150.00 a day going to make hits for Dead Eye and his uncle. He saved his first $150.00 so he could cop his own weed. It amazed him to see all that money at one time, and it was his own money. Dead Eye kind of like having DJ around. DJ had mo heart than sum of them older niggas. Whenever 5-0 would hit the block DJ never said shit.

Whenever they questioned him he wouldn't say shit. Besides he was out there just chilling and he didn't know what nobody else was doing because he minds his own business. He wasn't trying to get smart with them because it would only give them a reason to harass all of them even more. When Dead Eye saw 5-0 talking to DJ he was fore sure DJ was gone snitch but he didn't. At that very moment Dead Eye knew DJ was a real lil nigga. Shit like that made him keep DJ under his wings. Dead Eye was so use to calling him lil youngsta, lil nigga or lil dude, he didn't even know his real name. Once 5-0 left Dead Eye called out "Lil dude come here." DJ walked over to Dead Eye and replied "what up?" "What is yo real name?" Asked Dead Eye. "D'Wayne but they called me DJ." Replied DJ. "What's yo lil bro name?" Asked Dead Eye. "Desmond." Replied DJ. Dead Eye shook his head forward and said, "I never knew that that's why I asked." But Dead Eyes really wanted to know just in case he ever goes down and they snitch on him he will know exactly who it was that snitched.

Desmond walked on the block after 5-0 left looking for DJ. Dead Eye told DJ, "You got a lot of heart that's why I like having you around, "and most of all you don't snitch." "We already know snitches get stiches and end up in ditches for talking like bitches!" Spatted Desmond. Dead Eye busted out laughing and asked Desmond "what you know about that you ain't no street nigga?" Desmond replied "But I'm about to a street nigga!" Dead Eye told DJ and Desmond "around here you don't get stiches, but you end up in a ditches with outta doubt." Desmond shook his head real slow and said, "OKAY!" "We feel you!" Dead Eye told both DJ & Desmond "as long as we all got that understanding, we good with each other." DJ wasn't gone tell on nobody and Desmond always followed his lead. They wasn't gone bite the hand that's helping feed them. Just for not snitching Dead Eye gave DJ a pound of weed just for him and Desmond to make their own bread. At the ages of 13 & 12 DJ and Desmond knew how to break down and bag their own weed. Dead Eye told them they wasn't ready to make the real money yet. Desmond made him a quick $1500.00. He didn't have to touch what he saved up. All the money he made, he would take home and stash it.

DJ would spend a little here and there but he stashed majority of his loot too. They never took the weed home they kept it at Dead Eye's spot. When Desmond returned home to put his money with the rest of his stash, he recounted his money and some was missing. He knew his mom and siblings didn't touch it. The first person came to mind was Dre Bitch Ass. DJ was always gone and besides he had his own shit. DJ & Desmond barely saw each other until nighttime. Desmond wanted to confront Dre, but now at the age of 12 it wasn't much he could do, and it wasn't much DJ could do he had just turned 13. He couldn't go to his mom because she would want to know how he get so much money. Their mom was working odds and end jobs nothing persistent, and not enough to make ends meet.

DJ would give her a lil money to put toward the bills. DJ wanted to tell Desmond about his new hustle. He didn't know how things was gone turn out, so he stayed lo-key til the time was right. Desmond knew DJ was giving their mom like $50.00 every other day. The rent was only $200.00 a month, but he couldn't understand why they received and eviction notice. Desmond took it upon himself to call the landlord Mr. Cassidy, and act like he was calling for his mom. He wanted to see how far behind she was. Mr. Cassidy told Desmond she was behind 4 months in rent and if she didn't pay him by the end of the day all their belongings would be put out. Mr. Cassidy told Desmond he gave her a 30-day notice last month. Desmond asked Mr. Cassidy if he bring him $2000 over today can they stay there. Mr. Cassidy agreed but told Desmond his mom couldn't be late anymore. He needs his rent paid by the 5th of each month no later.

Desmond went down to the block to holla at DJ to see if he had half, because if they got evicted it's a strong possibility they all would go to foster care. DJ was nowhere to be found so Desmond went back to the crib grabbed the $2000.00 from his stash and jumped on his bike and road over to Mr. Cassidy's house to pay him. Desmond went back on the block after leaving Mr. Cassidy's house to make up what he just paid out. Dead Eye wasn't on the block. Knowing him he was probably laid up somewhere with one of his bitches. The only time Dead Eye ain't on the block is if he is laid up in sum pussy. Desmond knew he was young as hell, but being around Dead Eye and his uncle LOC he learned a lot about the streets and how to survive. Desmond knew he was ready to step it up a notch. He was still gone sale his weed, but he knew that if he messed with the white (hard) he would make his money 10x faster. He wanted to talk to DJ before he jumped right into it. He knew the consequences would be a lot harsher if he ever got caught selling the white.

DJ walked up on the block, DJ had a key to get in the spot. Desmond hollered at DJ and told him what he was thinking about doing and showed him the rent receipt on how much he had to pay Mr. Cassidy so they wouldn't get put out. DJ broke down and told Desmond he was already selling the white, he didn't want to tell him because he thought he would tell on him. Desmond looked at DJ in his eyes and said "Bro we all we got." "I would never snitch on you." Desmond told DJ he wanted to think about it first before he talked to Dead Eye about it. DJ went into his pocket and handed Desmond his $2000.00 back. When DJ pulled out all at money from both of his pockets Desmond couldn't believe he had just counted 8 stacks in front of him. Desmond was still gone sell his weed, but he knew he could double his money off the white. Desmond really thought all DJ was selling was weed he wanted to pull DJ in with him, but he had already stepped his shit up.

Desmond knew he had to put a plan into motion and he had to do it quick. Once he put his plan into motion he needed to holla at Dead Eye to see if he was down to go for it. Desmond told DJ "if it wasn't for you Bro, I wouldn't even know Dead Eye." "We all we got to the sky blows up!" DJ looked at Desmond and said, "it's always gone be F.O.E {family over everything}." While it was still summer the boys wanted to make as much loot as they could. DJ's phone ranged so he jumped on his bike to make a hit. They wanted to make sure they had gear for school and their siblings had gear for school too. The thought of making more money kept penetrating Desmond's mind. It was killing him just thinking about what he could do what all that money. He knew him and DJ would make a killing together. Desmond sat there for a few hours thinking to himself.

He then jumped on his bike to go find DJ because he needed to holla at him some more. Desmond road down on the West End and found DJ shooting sum hoop. He yelled over to DJ and told him he needed to holla at him real quick. DJ shot the ball and told them to give him a few he had to holla at his lil bro. Desmond told DJ "look bro you already know mom is barely working and Dre don't help do shit, we barely have anything." "Mom has really changed she ain't looking for no job or shit." "So it's up to us to do what we gotta do." "Like what?" Asked DJ. "I'm ready to make sum real bread so we can get ahead." Replied Desmond. "I got u lil bro." "We gone do this." Replied DJ. DJ told Desmond he been making some real money. He had been running errands for Dead Eye and once he saw how much he was making off the white he decided to do it to. So he took his money he made off the weed and bought him some white to flip that. DJ told Desmond he don't even sale weed anymore he sale straight white now.

Desmond felt some type of way hearing DJ say that, because he hid it from him the entire time. Although Desmond still wants to sale his weed because he has loyal customers. All that time Desmond thought DJ was still selling weed and cutting grass to use as a cover-up. DJ told Desmond he started selling the white for LOC. DJ said he had been selling a 200 count for LOC a day. DJ said he told LOC & Dead Eyes don't say anything to him because he didn't want anyone to find out. Hearing DJ say that pissed Desmond off because they were brothers and he felt like DJ trusted other people before he trusted him. "I'm sorry bro!" "I didn't want mom, Aunt Tracey or Granny to find out about it." DJ told Desmond. "Look bro do any of them know we sell weed?" "So why would you think I would tell anything else?" Replied Desmond. Desmond reminded DJ he was broke from paying Mr. Cassidy off until he gave him his money back. "Bro!" "I wanna use that to flip so I could get back on." "I still got a ½ pound of weed left but I'm ready to change sum shit up." Spatted Desmond. DJ was a little pissed knowing he had been giving his mom money and she hasn't paid any bills with it. DJ looked at Desmond and said, "Fuck It!" "Bro let's get it!"

Desmond hugged his big bro and gave him sum daps and at that moment they both was ready to jump sum shit off. Desmond went back to the house to put his money up and make sure his lil sisters and brothers was good. Shelly their 11-year-old sister was making sure the little ones was straight. The other kids was getting tired of eating noodles and cereal every day. Sometimes they had to eat their cereal dry because there was no milk in the house. DJ came home a couple hours later with 4 pizzas for them to eat. Desmond ran out and got them some chips, candy, cookies and juice to go with their pizzas. He even bought the baby sum food to eat. Shelly didn't ask no questions she was just happy to be eating something different for once. "Where is mom so she can come eat?" Asked Desmond. "She's in her room where she always is." Replied Shelly. Desmond left her sum pizza on the nightstand by her bed because she was sleeping. He then, called out to his lil sister Destiny so she could come eat but she wasn't hungry. Shelly told Desmond and DJ that Destiny hadn't really been or drinking anything. DJ called out for Destiny telling her to come eat, all kids love pizza, juice, candy, chips and cookies. She still didn't bulge. So he just left it by the bed hoping she would eat it. 10 minutes later Dre came home.

He didn't speak or say shit to anybody; he just walked up to the room. Three minutes later Dre comes downstairs eating a slice of pizza Desmond left for his mom. That's the kind of shit that pissed Desmond and DJ off. They just didn't know what to do about it. They knew their mom loved his no good ass. After everyone had eaten DJ & Desmond jumped on their bikes and bounced, they was on a straight paper chase from that point on. They had each other's back no matter what. DJ knew the only two niggas in the streets had their backs was Dead Eye and LOC. Especially if some bullshit jumped off in the streets. Motherfuckers didn't fuck with Dead Eye and LOC in the streets. They were like Drug Lords to them niggas out there. Dead Eye had everybody scared of him he stood about 5'10" Carmel coated complexion, with a medium muscle tone build. He was well known because of his glass eye. LOC & Dead Eye was around the same height, LOC was just a couple of inches taller. His skin was a tad bit darker that Dead Eye's. He stood about 6'0" with long colored tip dreads. LOC had everybody scared of him because he did a long bid in the joint, and the streets heard about his hands. In jail they said that nigga hands was lethal.

Dead Eye lost his eye when he was around 13. About the same age as DJ & Desmond is now. He intervened in a domestic dispute between his mother and her boyfriend. After he killed Dead Eye's mom in front of him he shot Dead Eye in the face before turning the gun on himself. After Dead Eye was released from the hospital he went from one foster home to another. Dead Eye's mother had a serious drug addiction. She sold pussy to feed her habit. His dad went to prison when he was 8 years old for murder. Dead Eye's always thought by his dad going to prison

16

lead to his mom's drug addiction. She fell into a deep depression after her left. His dad use to always write him, but once he went into the system his dad lost contact with him.

The last thing Dead Eye's remember his dad saying to him in a letter was when he got older he would tell him the truth behind his prison sentence and why he had to leave him. LOC couldn't get custody of Dead Eye because of his prior felony conviction. LOC was in prison on a drug charge when his sister was killed. So he had his baby moma Porsha to fight for custody of Dead Eye. Although Porsha had her own two kids by LOC to raise while he was in and out of jail. Dead Eye was 15 around the time Porsha was granted custody of him. By the time Dead Eyes turned 18 Porsha kicked him out of her house. He started following into LOC's footsteps. Ever since then Dead Eyes been on his own. LOC got out of prison when Dead Eye's was 26. Porsha had packed up and left town, so Dead Eyes had to be there for his uncle LOC til he got on his feet. Dead Eyes never had nothing more than misdemeanor charges. Dead Eye always had lil niggas running his packages for him so he wouldn't get caught with the shit. They knew if he found out they told on him and didn't carry their own weight they would come up stankin. Dead Eye's and LOC was running them streets. Once LOC saw how Dead Eye's was out there getting it.

He had a few 5-0's and a couple of federal agents paid off they was gone be good. As long as the couple of government agents was working with them they knew how to make their moves. It was still a few dick head cops that didn't like LOC from previous run in's but he never tripped over them. All they had to do was sit back chill and let the lil young motherfuckers do it for them. Out of all the runners they had they couldn't figure out why they went the extra mile for DJ & Desmond. Dead Eye always have said they're the realest lil niggas he's ever seen and they had heart more than them so called real niggas on the streets. LOC responded and said "Hell Yeah!" Dead Eye turned to LOC and said "unc they love making that cash." One day Dead Eye's asked DJ why him and Desmond would rather work the streets than go to school and get an education.

17

So they can become something in life. DJ responded with a nonchalant attitude: "we got bills to pay, and five other siblings that's depending on us right now." Dead Eye's looked at DJ and said, "I respect you lil nigga, but don't let this street shit get the best of yall." "The streets will be the first to break you and fuck you up." Dead Eyes told Desmond to have a seat next to his brother so he could talk to them. Dead Eye's rubbed the hair on his chin and took a moment to think. He looked at both of them and said "I got a lot of love for you lil niggas, but the streets is the devil, money is powerful, and drugs is an addiction." "When you put all that together you end up meeting your maker or inside them walls." Desmond didn't quite get what point he was trying to make. He turned to DJ and asked him what he had meant by that. DJ responded and said, "Desmond!" "Once you get addicted to drug money it becomes your habit, money becomes your power." "When you have money you feel like you don't want or need shit from other people." "Being in the streets leads to selling drugs because you are making dis honest money, and it can lead up to you going to jail or dead because you can't trust everybody." Well that was his version of what he thought it meant.

Desmond looked at DJ and said "ohhhhhh!" "I got it now!" Desmond turned to Dead Eye and said, "I just want to make some money to support my family." Dead Eye look at Desmond and said "yeah we all start out that way, but then other shit happens when you let money control you." Dead Eye told the boys "as long as yall stay under me and LOC wings yall gone be good." DJ shook his head and gave Dead Eye and fist bump and told him "me and bro here til the end." Dead Eye just couldn't believe how much loyalty these two lil niggas had. Desmond responded and said "its death before disloyalty and dis honor!" It fucked LOC up to hear that come from such as young nigga. That made Dead Eye and LOC fuck with them more than anybody else. They was all about making their bread. Everybody else was on sum ol' trick off shit with them hoes. One thing LOC instilled in them was never to get high of their own shit, as long as they remembered that they would stack money. Desmond and DJ decided that when school started they would still attend school to keep the officials off their mom's ass. By the end of the summer they made enough money to buy all the kids clothes, shoes, and supplies for school. They made sure the younger ones that wasn't in school had day-care. The house was stocked with food so the kids could eat breakfast before school and come home to food. Over the next few years they continued to go to school and still stack money. Life was started to become good for them and their siblings.

Chapter 3

By the ages of 15 & 16. Desmond and DJ had saved up a total of 20,000.00 together. The both of them were in disbelief, they had never seen that much money at onetime and could actually called it theirs. Moma Tanya and Tracey thought Talonda was back to her old self because the kids were looking descent again and food was being kept in the house. They didn't ask any questions they were just happy to see smiles on the kids' faces. In Talonda's twisted mind she actually thought they were making all that money doing odd jobs for people around the neighborhood. She really didn't care her bills were getting paid. Christmas was approaching very quickly. DJ knew his mom wasn't gone put shit under the tree for the kids or if she would even put a tree up. DJ had Dead Eye to take him to get his brothers and sisters some Christmas toys all he wanted to do was give them a Christmas they would never forget.

Desmond and DJ put up $750.00 a piece and got the kids sum clothes and toys. Dead Eye even put up $500 for the lil youngsters because he had so much love for DJ & Desmond. Dead Eye didn't have kids of his own, but he always looked out for the neighborhood kids. He knew first-hand what it was like not to have shit. DJ bought the kids a 7ft. white Christmas tree with all the colorful trimmings so Shelly could utilize her time decorating since she loves things of that nature. The boys never knew how to cook and they knew their mom wasn't going to cook, so they asked Dead Eye if they gave him the money would he order them Christmas Dinner from the restaurant down on 4th street. Dead Eye told them to keep their money he would have one of his bitches put something nice together for them. DJ and Desmond was very relieved to have gotten everything out the way for Christmas.

They knew they had just spent a lot bread and they had to make it back up. Christmas was in about two weeks everything was in place and squared out the way for them. They were so use to going to their grandmother's house for the holidays, for once they wanted everyone to come to their house, and they made sure everyone had a gift to open even if they didn't themselves. They knew Tracey and Moma Tanya was gone get all of them something too. Christmas day was finally here, DJ gave Shelly and the kids their outfits to put on for Christmas and even bought their mom and outfit for Christmas. Desmond woke their mom to comb the kid's hair and make sure everyone was together before their grandmother, grandfather and Auntie came over. Dead Eye stopped by to drop off the food his lil bitch prepared for them. DJ wanted Dead Eye to stay for dinner so he told him to call LOC over so they can come and have dinner with them also because they were family to them. Dead Eye was cool with eating with the family, DJ knew his grandmother and aunt will question who were LOC and Dead Eye.

He had the perfect answer for them when they asked. He was gone tell them they had their own construction company and they pay them to do odd and end jobs. Auntie Tracy wouldn't fall for it, her nosey ass was gone know they were lying they just hoped she didn't ruin the holiday by saying they look like suspected drug dealers. Shelly prepared the table with all the food before opening gifts. She asked everyone to make a circle around the table and hold hands so they could bless the food. DJ noticed his lil sister Kelly wasn't out there with them. He asked Shelly where was Kelly she looked around and said, "I thought she was out here with everyone." "I'll go get her." Kelly is now 8 years old but ever since she had turned 3 she acted like nothing really interest her any more. Everyone blamed Talonda for that because she wasn't spending anytime with her kids like she use too. DJ asked Shelly if Kelly was ok, she shook her head and said "yeah she is." Moma Tanya told DJ that Kelly was ok she will eventually come around. Everyone sat at the table and began to laugh, talk and eat their dinner. The little kids were ready to open their gifts so everyone finished eating so they could see what Santa brought the family. Mama Tanya also noticed Dre was nowhere to be found the entire day. She figured he wouldn't show up because he didn't care for her or Tracy. The moment he found out they were doing Christmas at Talonda's house he got pissed and left. No one cared they ain't want his ol' leaching ass there anyways.

Talonda is the only person who gives a shit about his no good ass, the kids was so happy with the gifts they received. Shelly loved her knew laptop, clothes and shoes. Mama Tracy, Aunt Tanya loved their perfume gift sets. When Shelly handed her mama her gift, she opened it and loved her knew make-up set, she use to always put on make-up before she went to work. The kids knew how much their mom loved her make-up, but ever since Dre came into the picture she don't wear make-up or clothes anymore. DJ hugged his mom and told her to go to the bathroom and put some make-up on for old time sake like she use too. Talonda smiled and said, "Ok baby just for you." As the family continued to enjoy their day, Aunt Tracy just had to ask Dead Eye and LOC how they knew her nephews. Dead Eye started to answer but he let LOC answer. LOC spatted, "I just help put a lil money in their pockets so they could take care of home." Desmond was noticing his Aunt Tracy kept her eyes on LOC not as if she didn't trust him but as if she was attracted to him. After all LOC did a long ass bid in the joint so he got out swollen as hell.

His arms was big as fuck. He looked like he would knock a nigga out with one light punch. Aunt Tracy knew LOC was really lying but she didn't say anything because she didn't have any proof. Everyone sat and watched a movie together and it started getting late so Dead Eye and LOC was about to bounce. Right before they got ready to leave LOC asked Tracy for her number. DJ was shocked that she gave it to him, when he told Desmond about it. Desmond told DJ that he kind of figured Aunt Tracy was into LOC by the way she kept conversing with him the entire night. Since they were on winter break from school, DJ and Desmond knew they had to makeup what they dropped out for Christmas. They was about to make sum drastic changes and they knew they needed cell phones so they could stay in contact. Dead Eye took them to get phones because they wasn't 18 yet. They was about to be gone every day, all day til they made back what they spent plus more. Besides they had to use LOC or Dead Eye's phone to call and check on Shelly and the kids.

They thought celebrating the holiday would bring their mom back to her senses but it didn't. Once everybody left she went and locked herself back into her room. DJ came across a government phone off the streets, so he bought it for Shelly to use in case of an emergency and if anything ever happens to the house phone. Now they started to feel a lil more comfortable being gone all day. Over the next few months DJ & Desmond continued to stack bread. For sum odd reason the money was starting to go to DJ's head. He was about to turn 17 in May and he wanted to do it big for his birthday. He really wanted to get sum pussy for the first time. He would see all these big booty bitches come over for Dead Eye. Hell a few times he even heard one of the bitches getting the shit fucked outta her. All he could say to himself is when he got ahold to him a lil bitch he was gone fuck the shit out her ass. He would hear them in the room moaning so loud, that he had to grab his own dick as if he was in there making her moan like that. He always dreamed of making a women sound like that since puberty kicked in and from watching all that late night porn on Cinemax.

For his birthday he wanted to get a couple of tricks for him and Desmond. He mentioned to his lil Bro Desmond about his plans. At first Desmond was against it. Then he thought to himself very quickly. I wouldn't mind getting me sum head for the first time. His lil premature dick got hard instantly just from the thought. He turned to DJ with a huge smile on his face and said "hell yeah let's get two bitches one for you and one for me, and have our way with them." Then he thought about it and asked, "where would we take them DJ?" As he started to get anxious. The more they talked about it the more they was getting horny. DJ replied "we can see if LOC or Dead Eye can get us a couple of rooms for the night." "OK!" "But who are we going to take?" Asked Desmond. "I don't know as of yet." "I will mention it to LOC and Dead Eye and let them know what my plans are for my 17th birthday." Replied DJ. Desmond and DJ sat back and reminisced about what they night would be like if they had two bad ass bitches that will fuck & suck the shit outta them.

DJ decided to go ahead and tell LOC and Dead Eye about his birthday plans and to their surprise the both of them was cool with it. The day of DJ's birthday he & Desmond bought themselves sum fresh new fits, fresh new kicks, and got sum fresh haircuts. Dead Eye had one of his lil bitches rent a car for DJ in her name. Although DJ didn't have any driver's license, he still wanted him a rental so he could show stop for his 17th birthday. Desmond didn't even know DJ knew how to drive, but LOC taught him how to drive when he brought him under his wings. DJ was geeked and ready to see sum ass shaking that night. He made sure he had plenty of dollars that night cuz his first stop was the strip club. They wasn't worried about getting carded because LOC & Dead Eye had ties with the strip club owner. DJ learned a lot being around Dead Eye. Desmond was ready to step all the way out the box like DJ. It was still a lot they had to learn. Both boys got dressed and was ready to see what the night held for them. They couldn't believe how good they looked. They always looked descent but they knew they was the shit that night. Dead Eye made it happen for the lil niggas.

His one lil bitch rented them a white Audi with peanut butter insides and leather seats. Desmond noticed DJ was already starting to act a lil arrogant instantly. Desmond knew DJ was gone act a fool that night, but he made sure he had a nice lil stack on him to so he could make it rain on a few hoes. They stopped at the gas station on the way to the strip club so they could get them a box of rubbers to have on hand just in case they did get sum ass. LOC and Dead Eye stayed behind and let the fellas go handle their business, LOC made sure that would be a night they would never forget. When they arrived at "Strippers Nation" the most popular 24 hour strip club in the city. DJ wanted valet parking so they didn't have to walk too far. They had a VIP Booth and bottles already reserved and waiting for them when they walked through the door. They looked like sum straight up ballers. They had random bitches trying to chill, but DJ didn't want just no any random bitches in his booth. He wanted sum bad bitches around them that night. Desmond wasn't tripping as long as he got sum head and pussy that night.

DJ wanted to make a name for himself, he wanted to fuck one of the baddest bitches in the club, that wasn't quick to give that pussy up to just any ol' random ass nigga just because she was a stripper. Dead Eye had already looked out for them, and yes he made sure the both of them had sum bad ass bitches too. When Diamond Fox and Wet Wet came over to the booth their eyes lit up. They told them that a friend of theirs reserved for them to hang out with them and made sure they enjoyed their night. DJ was loving it he didn't know which one to pick because they both was bad as hell. Desmond had his eye on the red bone Diamond Fox. So DJ took Wet Wet. They had never seen two women with so much ass before. The ladies danced and gave the fellas lap dances all night and they made sure they tipped them real well.

Both of them was virgins so they was worried about if they could handle these advanced bitches because they was definitely sum freaks. They was popping their pussies in their faces so much it made them want to pull their thong string to the side and start licking their pussies right there. Although they never eaten pussy before they was ready to learn that night. Dead Eye had already given the ladies the heads up that this was the first time for both of them and to make it worth their wild. DJ popped open the bottle of Don P, he poured it down the center of Wet Wet's back and started to licking it off her spine it started making her horny because that was her spot. Whenever her back got licked it made her freaky instantly. Desmond was more so slapping Diamond Fox on her ass while she was popping it in his face.

Both ladies untied the string of their thongs and took them off, Wet Wet placed her thong around DJ's neck and Diamond Fox placed hers on Desmond's head. Then the ladies laid on the floor and started popping their pussies up in the air as DJ and Desmond looked mesmerized. DJ started rubbing his money up against Wet Wet's pussy and slapping her pussy with his dollars. Desmond said fuck rubbing the pussy with sum dollars. He rubbed Diamond Fox's pussy with his fingers. They scent of the Japanese Cheery Blossom smell from her pussy made his dick get instantly hard when he smelled his fingers. They were teasing DJ & Desmond so much they was ready to leave the strip club and go straight to the telly. They didn't put a dent in the fifth of white Henn cuz they were too focused on all the scattered ass and pussy in their faces. Desmond asked the ladies if they were ready to leave and go to the telly. Both ladies agreed they were ready.

They went to the back to get dressed so they could go and show the youngsters what grown women pussy was about. When they arrived at the telly they went straight to their rooms. Both ladies asked the men to wait outside why they get ready to put on a special show for them. The boys walked back to the car because they forgot their rubbers and by the time they arrived back to their rooms both ladies was standing in the hall way butt naked with just stiletto's on. Their rooms was on point they had champagne, and rose petals laying around the Jacuzzi. All DJ could do was think of how Dead Eye hooked it up for his 17th birthday. They felt like grown men for once. Desmond and his girl for the night went down to DJ's room so they could have a toast for the night and both ladies could dance one last time for the night. Desmond ran back to the car to get the bottle of white Henn they didn't get to finish in the club. So they could be nice and buzzed and ready for whatever the night had to offer.

The ladies was actually enjoying themselves with DJ and Desmond. They were all showing each other a good time. The fellas didn't know who was hornier them or the ladies, because they started doing sum real freaky shit. They were sucking on their fingers as if they were sucking their dicks. Desmond decided he wanted more of a private show from his chick so they went back to their room and left DJ and Wet Wet alone in their room. The minute Desmond and Diamond Fox left DJ's room Wet Wet started gropping and rubbing on DJ. She started licking the crouch of his pants with her long thin frail tongue as he began to get stiff in the dick area. Wet Wet couldn't believe that was all DJ she was feeling up against his pants as she licked and licked. She decided to unzip his pants so she could become up close and personal with his man hood.

She looked up at DJ as she licked around the tip of his dick and saying to him how she never seen so many inches on such a young kid before. She gripped his dick with her hand because the width was so overwhelming to her. She looked up at DJ once again telling him she can see its gone be a very good night, because she is going to have so much fun slurping, slobbing and gagging on all his meat. DJ allowed her to undress him slowly as she teased him with her tongue licking all over his body. Whenever she licked his nipples it made him feel weaker and weaker. She was trying to dominate DJ because she knew it was his first time ever having sex, but he stood his ground like a real nigga. Before DJ knew it she was deep throating him and making all kinds of slobbering noises that started sounding like music to his ears. Every time she went deeper and deeper her nose would touch his navel and she made a certain moan that sent DJ over the roof.

He was feeling his soul leave his body for a few seconds. DJ was starting to realize why dudes talked about getting head so much, because it was a feeling that felt so good. As he stood there while she was on her knees looking up at him while she sucked and sucked the life out of him his back was starting to get numb. Meanwhile a few doors down Desmond was getting almost the same treatment. Desmond couldn't resist how fat and juicy Diamond Fox's pussy looked he just wanted to taste it to see if it tasted as good as it looked. Although Desmond was a year younger that DJ was. Diamond Fox hadn't seen such a big dick on a sixteen year old. Desmond started sucking and slurping on Diamond fox's pussy making her shiver and her body tremble. He remembered how they were doing it on the porn they watched on Cinemax and gave her his all. He put her legs over his shoulder as he licked around her ass hole and back to her clitoris, her knees were starting to shake even more, as she grabbed his head and pushed his face in her pussy. He turned her over and put her ass up as he licked and penetrated her ass hole with his finger she started moaning louder and louder.

Saying in a very soft sexy tone "Ohhhhh!" "Desmond don't stop!" The more she called his name to more he licked with aggression. Diamond said in another soft toned voice, "Desmond please stick your dick in me and fuck me." Desmond knew he was doing a good job because she was begging to feel his dick inside of her. He pulled out his rubbers to put one on. But Diamond wanted to feel his fresh meat inside of her. Desmond knew about STD's and he knew he wasn't ready for no baby so he told her he couldn't give it to her raw but in due time she will feel the freshness of his meat. He put the rubber on and began to slide his dick in her tight pussy inch by inch. Every inch he gave her felt so good to him and her, he was ready to pound away on her pussy but he wanted to fuck her as if he knew what he was doing. He was just starring at her ass as she was bent over while he was fuck her and putting his finger just an inch in her ass, she was getting wetter and wetter.

The more he pumped the more her juices was dripping from her pussy. He would pull out and start licking it some more then put it back in. She was loving it as she screamed and moaned his name with every stroke he gave her. Desmond loved smacking and gripping all that ass that was in his face. He pulled out and told Diamond Fox he wanted her to ride him. As she began to sit on his dick she tightened up her pussy walls and slid onto him nice and slowly while holding his arms down in a restraint position. Desmond was loving it as she gripped his dick and rode him in a circular motion. She started to scream louder and louder and she started to cum on his dick. Desmond hadn't nutted yet so she took the rubber off and began to suck him until she sucked all the cum he could produce at that moment out of him.

She spitted his cum on him and licked it back off leaving no residue of it on his body. Back in DJ's room Wet Wet was ready to see what DJ had to offer. She took out the condom the wrapper put it in her mouth and rolled it down DJ's dick with her lips and preceded to ride him. She was giving DJ her all, putting him in position he had never seen before in all the porn he watched. DJ never knew a person could do a back bend while riding your dick at the same time. Her pussy was so deep that while she was riding him you couldn't see a trace of his dick. She made sure all his meat was inside of her. As she pounced up and down on him she was moaning so loud he thought the people in the other rooms could hear her. He couldn't believe he was hearing such an advanced woman moan so loud.

DJ wanted her to see him perform so he told her to lay on her back in the missionary position as he lifted her legs over his shoulders and began to fuck her slowly. Wet Wet didn't like getting slow fucked she liked for you to ram the dick in her pussy. She likes fucking aggressively, she wanted DJ to choke her, slap her and take charge of that pussy like it was his own private pussy. She was telling DJ how to fuck her because she knew what would make her cum real good. DJ flipped her on her stomach and began to fuck her with the intention of making her feel all of him. He was fucking her so good the rubber busted, as he was about to put another one on, Wet Wet said, "don't worry about putting another on, I wanna suck the cum out that dick and taste every drop of it." She sucked DJ's dick for about five more minutes and he began to squirt his juices in her mouth and on her face as she licked the remaining of the cum off the tip of his dick. She continued to suck his dick til he was begging her to stop. DJ's body became limp as a noodle after her nutted. He couldn't do anything else but fall asleep. After the boys fell asleep the ladies left and went home also.

The next day the boys were so drained from such a wild ass night they didn't wanna do shit. They left the hotel and DJ let out an outburst "MANNNNN!" "That was the best birthday ever!" Desmond looked over at DJ shook his head and said "hell fucking yeah!" "My nigga!" As tired as they were they refused to have a nice ass rental and don't do shit. They went home showered changed clothes and road around hitting blocks like they was the shit. Before they knew it all the little young bitches around their ages that wasn't trying to fuck with them before started dick riding. When they seen them riding through the hood in a nice ass Audi. They was trying to get their attention and throw pussy at them. Since they lost their virginity to sum grown ass women they felt like it was nothing them lil young bitches in the hood could do for them. They made sure all them lil young bitches and niggas that use to talk about them in school saw them. Everybody wanted to fuck with them now. One thing they learned from LOC and Dead Eye was to keep their circle small. They had each other so they didn't need to fuck with no one else unless it was Dead Eye and LOC. Bringing other motherfuckers in their circle could become a problem for them. If they stuck together they would be good. Everything was in order at their crib finally. Their brothers and sisters were good. They felt like it was time for them to take over the streets in Gary, Indiana.

Chapter 4

Shelly called DJ's phone, she wanted to know why their mom was looking so bad. DJ and Desmond knew there was a huge change in their mom's appearance. All DJ could do was tell her not to worry they will take care of whatever the problem was. He didn't have an honest answer for her, because he didn't know himself what the problem was. DJ and Desmond wanted to make sure they was good and could manage before they focused on their mom. They knew selling drugs was wrong and it wasn't the answer to their problems, but it was helping them out a lot. They wasn't too focused on the consequences at that moment. They were only focused on getting money and making ends meet for the family. Seeing other dope fiends in the hood, they already knew what drugs did to people and they had a strong gut feeling their mom was on drugs. She was cool til she started fucking with Dre.

She was never good at picking her nigga's but he was the worse she has ever been with. He didn't care about her or her kids. He had a free roof over his head and he could get free pussy when he wanted it. They didn't pay any attention to her when they were younger they was too busy trying to be kids. Shelly called DJ's phone back and told him something was wrong with Kelley, she stopped eating again and all she would do is lay around and have tears in her eyes as if she wanted to cry. Shelly tried talking her mom into taking her to the doctor, but all she did was

31

blow it off. Nothing mattered to Talonda anymore not even her own kids. DJ told Shelly to call Moma Tanya so she could come see what was wrong with Kelley. She called Moma Tanya to come over to the house she explained to her what was going on and how her mom wouldn't get up to check and see if she was ok. Moma Tanya rushed over to Talonda's house to see if everything was ok with Kelley.

She wasn't running a temp or anything. Moma Tanya thought it could be the huge change in Talonda that affected her. Moma Tanya sat there for a while and everything seemed ok so far wasn't none of the kids ill or anything so she went on home. DJ told Desmond what Shelly told him about Kelley. Desmond was closer to Kelley because he took up more time with her and spoiled her a lot. He decided to take her for ice cream so he could talk to her, but the plan didn't work. At the same time DJ was praying he didn't drop any dope around the house and Kelley got ahold of it thinking it was candy or something. All of a sudden she became so distant from everyone. She spent most of her time laying around, she would barely eat anything. Moma Tanya went out and bought her sum canned supplements for her to drink to put nutrients back into her little frail body. Shelly only had a twin size bed but if it made Kelley feel better to sleep with her she was ok with that. Desmond was so worried about Kelley that he kept bugging DJ and asking him if he thought she would be ok. DJ told Desmond he thought Kelley was just seeking attention from their mom.

Desmond told DJ he felt like "ever since Dre came along, their mom just forgotten about everything." Desmond knew his mom had went downhill, she stopped putting on clothes and combing her hair, even putting on makeup. She used to love her makeup. She don't even care how the kids look or even take the time out to see if they've eaten or anything. DJ responded, "yeah I know Des". "That's why it's on us to do what we got do to make show we all good". DJ and Desmond decided to stay out all night to make as much money as they could. Although DJ wanted to find him another older bitch to trick off with in the meantime. DJ always kept him a hype car so he could move around when he wanted too. DJ dropped Desmond off at the spot and told him he had a run to make. He rode around hitting a few blocks trying to make a few dollars and find him a bitch to give him sum head. He pulled up on Crayton Blvd. to chill for a minute, this one thick ass bitch walked up to the car. It was his mother's old friend Tootie, whom he always looked at like a godmother to him and his sibling, before she fell out with his mom. No matter how much dope that bitch smoked, she was still thick ass hell, and she kept herself looking good. If you didn't know her you wouldn't believe she got high because she was finer than a motherfucker.

DJ always had a crush on Tootie when he was a lil boy despite her being like another mother to him. When she approached DJ's car she asked him what he was on. DJ replied, "shit just chilling looking for something to get into." Tootie asked DJ what he was trying to get into. DJ didn't hesitate to say he was looking for him a lil trick to get him some head from. DJ didn't feel bad about it being Tootie that would give him some head. In his mind he felt like if that bitch would smoke some dope, she would do anything. Tootie went around to the other side of the car jumped in the passenger seat and told DJ to pull around to the alley. She preceded to give DJ sum head real quick, once she was done he gave her a sack and she went on her way. DJ use to have the up most respect for Tootie now to him she was just another bitch out there on the streets. DJ done got his first piece of pussy for his birthday now all he wanna do is trick off with these bitches. He knew he needed to stay focused, but he was tryna get that one feeling Wet Wet gave him when she sucked and fucked him. He just knew Tootie was gone top him off real good but she wasn't all that.

Wet Wet sucked his dick like she enjoyed doing what she do. DJ was starting to get like Dead Eye every chance he got he was trying to trick off with him a lil bitch. One thing for sure he made sure he made sho he stacked his bread first. DJ went back to the spot with Desmond to see what was popping over there. Dead Eye had been MIA lately. Desmond asked LOC "what the hell Dead Eye been on lately?" LOC told him, "he act like he in love with that one bitch that had all them damn kids." Desmond asked LOC with a grin on his face "what the hell he want a bitch with a lot of kids for?" LOC said, "shidd the bitch get high and he let that bitch suck his dick, now every time you turn around this nigga tryna go stick his dick down her throat." Desmond asked LOC if he ever met her. LOC responded, "hell naw I don't be wanting to meet them bitches he fucking with out there." "Those bitches might talk too damn much for me."

Desmond and DJ busted out laughing. DJ said, "while he was still laughing hell yeah that's what I'm talking about a bitch that will suck the life out a nigga." Desmond said, "shidd I want more than just my dick sucked." LOC laughed at both of them and said, "I see yall finally starting to grow yall lil young asses up now." LOC wasn't the type to fall in love with them bitches, he had one bitch he was in love with and she left him while he was in prison and moved out of town and he hasn't heard from her since the last letter she wrote him telling him she was leaving. LOC would just fuck bitches here and there and move around on they ass. DJ was gradually starting to act like Dead Eye, but the more his ass fucked around with Tootie the more it seemed like his ass was starting to get stupid for that bitch. Tootie was a hustler despite her getting high. DJ would get a kick out of seeing Tootie sprinkle a lil powder on the tip of his dick and snort it off. For sum reason every time she did that his dick would stay hard as fuck for hours. That shit would make him want to fuck all night.

It made her want to fuck all night too. Tootie didn't care shit about her been knowing him his entire life. All she cared about was that lil nigga had sum money and sum good dick for his age. DJ was starting to wild out, so Desmond became the protector over his siblings because DJ was too busy wrapped up in his own shit. Tootie ass stayed at the Poker joint getting those old cats for their money. DJ liked how she hustled it made him feel like she was sort of a female version of him. This nigga started riding around the hood with Tootie like she was his main bitch or sum shit. It wasn't that though Tootie was down to get money also. She wasn't like the usual dope fiends in the hood. She knew if she stayed in the poker joint she could hit an easy lick, because them older niggas was to focus on how good she looked and, DJ thought everybody in the hood knew Tootie got high, but they didn't. They thought she was just a hoe because her ass was always in the streets. You couldn't look at her and tell she got high because that bitch stayed on point, she kept her hair and nails done and she stayed geared up. That bitch didn't have no car but she would walk miles in them heels.

Tootie told DJ to take her up to the Poker house on West Point Dr., so she could make her sum quick cash. DJ drove her up there and he wanted to go in with her, but she just wanted him to drop her off and told him she'll call him when she's ready. She didn't want DJ to know she did a lil more than just gank them older niggas out their money. She did whatever she had to do to get that money. They loved when she came because that was the only night they got to see sum ass and play strip poker. She would play a few games with the fellas to get them nice and ready and let them feel like they making a lil money. She would put on a lil strip show for them and let them play with her pussy a lil bit and sometimes lick on it if they liked. They just couldn't fuck unless they wanted to drop out sum Benjamin's.

Once she had them right where she wanted them, thinking with their dick and not their brain she would play another round so she can get paid and split. They were so amped up and wanted her to do more. She had a few tricks up her sleeve. She told the one with the most money if she won the next game he had to empty his pockets. He looked at the other gentleman and laughed and said, "Well I doubt if I'll be emptying my pockets." "If you just so happen to win I will empty my pockets and tongue kiss that kitty the right way for you too." Tootie looked at him very nonchalant and said "fuck it lets play!" She let him deal the cards; he clearly didn't realize he was playing with a bitch that had more street since than he thought. If this bitch ain't know nothing else she knew a good hustle.

He kept smirking and licking his lips, he then said to Tootie "so say if you just so happens to lose which you will." "I guess I will get to treat you like my own lil personal slut for the day." She grinned and said "just put yo money where yo dentures is." "Old man!" He grinned back at Tootie and said "well get to stripping cuz I got a full house Triple Ace and two Kings". She winked her right eye and said "empty them old ass pockets motherfucker and keep yo wack ass head!" "I got a Royal Flush, Ace, 10 Jack, and King!" Tootie always kept them cards on her, but they be busy fantasizing over her body and focusing on tryna fuck if she loss. They never pay attention that she sits in the exact same spot. Once she walks in the door she plants her cards, play around with them for a minute and go in for the kill. She made her a quick $4500 in every bit of two hours. DJ had been giving her sum of that young meat she didn't even want to trick off with the older cats no more. Tootie done fucked a lot of niggas in her time but for some reason she liked fucking with DJ.

She never imagined fucking with someone she always looked at as a son. She was actually starting to have a lil feelings for DJ. But not enough to where she won't fuck another nigga to get sum bread. Tootie thought she was DJ's first piece of pussy, but little did she know Wet Wet took his innocence and gave that nigga a moment he would never forget. That was the best pussy DJ ever had. He started fucking with other bitches but none on them amounted to Wet Wet. Tootie started stepping her game up, she started working them pussy walls right and gripping his dick just like he liked it. She was gripping him so good he felt like he was trying to break out of cuffs. Desmond was noticing DJ was tricking off a lil too much with Tootie. Whenever he tried talking to him about it. He would say it was his money and he hustle for his own shit. Desmond was starting to feel like he was losing his own brother to dat bitch. DJ was starting to change a lot.

He was spending more and more time with Tootie or them other bitches in the streets. DJ thought Desmond was jealous because he wasn't getting pussy like he was. DJ was starting to forget about the real reason why they were in the game anyways. They were supposed to be doing this to support the family. Every day Desmond was starting to feel like he was carrying all the weight on his shoulders. He was the only person making sure food was in the house and the bills were getting paid. All DJ was worried about was fucking off with Tootie trick ass and them other bum ass bitches. He was really starting to piss Desmond off. Desmond tried to get Dead Eye and LOC to talk to him, not saying that it would work but it was worth the try. LOC reached out to DJ because he was the oldest of everybody. Dead Eye never responded which Desmond knew he probably wouldn't because he was wrapped up in his own shit. Dead Eye was starting to change himself. Dead Eye never brought his girl around, he would just disappear for days without a trace, hell they didn't know if he was with the same one everyday cuz he had so many. He wouldn't return texts or calls.

Shelly called Desmond and told him he needs to come home it was very important. She wouldn't tell him why she was hysterical and crying telling him to hurry and come home. Desmond tried calling DJ so he could meet him at the crib, but he didn't answer his damn phone as usual. Desmond made it home in 15 minutes flat. He ran into the house to see what was going on with Shelley. He ran started to yell for Shelley when he got in the house, she didn't respond. He ran upstairs and found Shelly in her room holding her lil sister Destiny. They were both crying their eyes out. Desmond became hysterical and at the same time trying catch his breath and ask what was wrong at eh same time. Shelly looked at Desmond and said with her voice shaking from crying, Destiny told me Dre had been touching her in her private area and making her do bad things to him.

Desmond dropped to his knees in disbelief. He looked up at Shelly trying to hold his tears back from the anger he just built up and asked Shelly. "What the fuck did you just say Shelly?" Shelley repeated herself and said "its true Des, I know it is because he use to do the same thing to me!" "I was so scared to say anything because I didn't want nobody to get hurt!" Shelley went on to tell him one night I got up to use the bathroom and I saw him lying in the bed with Kelley and Destiny. I knew he was doing something bad. He asked me what was I looking at and to go back to my room. Desmond asked Shelly had Dre been here. She said she hadn't seen Dre in a couple of weeks. It's not out of the ordinary he always disappears and come back. She said the last time he was there he accused mom of cheating, they argued and he left. Desmond was completely silenced all he could do was shake his head and hug all three of his lil sisters. He told them "he loved them and everything is going to be ok." "He told Shelly come lock the door he will be right back, and if Dre come don't open the door for him." Desmond kept calling DJ's phone it was going straight to voicemail. He called Dead Eye's phone and got no answer. The only person left to call was LOC. Desmond called LOC and told him he was walking down Trail Rd. and asked if he could come swoop him. He explained to LOC it was very important and he got a dilemma. He thought LOC could give him the best advice on how to handle to situation. Desmond didn't want to get the police involved.

He wanted to take care of that nigga on his own. Desmond wasn't a violent person but he would do whatever he had to do to protect his family. LOC went to swoop up Desmond so he could see what was up. Desmond asked him if he could take him to hit sum blocks while he try and clear his head a lil. LOC knew something was wrong because Desmond never sit in the car quiet. He either turning up the radio, rapping and bouncing to every song that comes on. He was just sitting in the car looking pissed off. LOC knew whatever it was it had to be serious because he had never seen Desmond zoned out like he was. One part of Desmond was ashamed to say something, and another part of him wanted to tell somebody. He wanted to talk to DJ first. He kept calling DJ but he didn't respond to any calls or texts. He was starting to worry that something happened to him. It wasn't like DJ to ignore him like that. DJ had to know it was something serious, because Desmond wouldn't be blowing up his phone like he was.

Chapter 5

Two days went by and Desmond still hadn't heard from DJ. He continued to ride through all the known areas with LOC looking for Dre, but no one had seen him in a few weeks. Finally DJ called Desmond to see what's been going on. Desmond was so pissed at DJ he just hung up on him. The entire time LOC was with Desmond he didn't have a clue what was going on with him. He knew Desmond was pissed but he didn't want to ask any questions, he felt like if he wanted him to know he'll tell him. DJ called Desmond phone and Desmond kept rejecting his calls. LOC decided to holla at Desmond and ask him what was up. Desmond replied, "what u mean?" LOC said, "Why da fuck you keep hanging up on yo bro like that nigga." LOC could see it all over Desmond's face that he was pissed off about something, and this was sum serious shit. His eyes were blood shot red, and he had the look of the devils' advocate written all over his face. Desmond took a deep breath and spatted, "This nigga Dre been molesting all my lil sisters and I'm gone kill his bitch ass when I see him!"

LOC know first-hand about how he felt, cuz he woulda did a full bid for trying to protect his sister too. The only difference was Desmond lil sisters are still here and able to tell their story. LOC felt his pain 100%. Desmond went on to repeat what Shelly had told him to LOC. The more Desmond talked the more LOC started to get pissed. Desmond told LOC

39

how DJ hadn't been responding to any of his calls nor has he been to the crib to check on the kids in days. LOC knew DJ would listened to him, so he told Desmond he will holla at DJ about all the bullshit he's been on. LOC told Desmond "we been up for damn near 48 hours and we barely eaten any damn thing." Desmond wasn't trying to hear that shit all he was thinking about was finding Dre and making an example out his ass. LOC grabbed Desmond by his shoulders and told him in a strong tone "you need to calm the fuck down lil nigga!" "We gone take care of all the bullshit but you got to be level headed about the shit!" "Nigga!" "I'm not tryna go back to the joint!" "Yo ass never been there!" "You don't know what the fuck it's like!" "I'm never scared to go back but if I don't have too, I won't!" "Now you need to pull yo ass together and let me think of how we gone play this bullshit out!"

Once Desmond knew he had somebody down with him. He started to feel a lil bit better. He listened to LOC and tried to calm down a little. "You see DJ ain't doing shit right now, so I hope you ain't depending on him to be there!" Spatted LOC. The more LOC talked to Desmond the more his eyes filled with water. LOC knew Desmond wasn't cut like that on the low, but he felt his pain. At the same time LOC saw a few niggas that wasn't cut like that get down so he wasn't gone second guess Desmond too much. When Desmond held his head up, he couldn't control the tears that rolled down his caramel cheeks. "LOC!" "I failed my sisters and DJ punk ass too busy tricking off with these bitches he don't even know what the fuck is going on!" "If he saw Shelly calling his phone he had to know it was something was wrong!" Said Desmond. LOC shook his head. "Just chill fool". "We got this". "It's definitely gone get handled". "I keep telling you", "I got you lil nigga". Spatted LOC. LOC drove Desmond back to the spot ordered them a pizza and tried to gather their thoughts together. The entire time Desmond really couldn't eat, all he could do was think. He was getting a headache from thinking so much. LOC couldn't really eat either, he was too busy thinking about his own sister he had lost.

The more he watched Desmond the more he started to think of all the should of's, could of's and would of's. He knew it was all a thought although he was wishing he could change the hands of time he knew it was just a hopeless thought. Desmond was noticing the huge change in DJ and he didn't start changing until he started fucking with Tootie kind of tuff. Although Tootie was like their godmother and also like an aunt to them he couldn't believe that she would start fucking with DJ like that. The more he thought about shit the more he got pissed. He started to break down all over again. DJ called Desmond's phone once again. LOC told Desmond to let him answer it. LOC asked DJ where was he at. DJ responded, "just chillin right now." "Whats up?" LOC said "look here we got a serious situation going on and imma give yo lil bro back the phone so he can fill you in."

When Desmond got the phone and preceded to tell DJ what Shelly had just told him. DJ kept talking to other people and laughing on the phone like the shit was a fucking joke. Desmond was starting to get even more pissed. He just spatted out with a very loud tone "FUCK YOU DJ!" Then hung up the phone. LOC called DJ back and said in a very serious tone. "Look nigga get yo ass here right now and now I'm not playing!" "I just told yo ass this shit was serious and you on the fucking phone laughing and joking and not even fucking listening!" DJ had never heard the serious side of LOC so he knew he needed to get his ass there and quick. Tootie was tryna hang out some more. She put her two sense in tryna tell DJ he didn't have to listened to LOC he wasn't his fucking daddy. DJ knew LOC was serious though. He knew if Tootie said sum shit like that around LOC he would probably slap the shit out her ass and it wouldn't have been shit he could do to save her.

DJ dropped Tootie off at the lil Poker joint she always go to for a couple hours while he went to the spot to see what was going on. DJ walked in all loud and shit, then flopped his frail ass on the couch. He looked over at Desmond and said "what's up Des what you been on?" Desmond looked at DJ and shook his head. It was complete silence until DJ decided he wanted to make stupid ass noises. Desmond looked over at DJ and said "WHAT THE FUCK IS WRONG WITH YOU DUDE!" In a high pitch but strong tone. LOC gave DJ the side eye because he knew he was tripping too. Within 10 minutes DJ nodded off. LOC looked over at Desmond and said "I could be wrong but I think his ass been tooting that shit". Desmond said "Naw LOC!" "I know he's smarter than that." "That was one of the first things yall taught us when yall introduced us into the game." LOC responded to Desmond "look youngster I been out on these streets since you was just a liquid baby in yo daddy's nut sack." "I know how motherfuckers who toot powder get to tripping." "Either that or his ass fucking with that water." Desmond didn't want to believe DJ was capable of fucking with that shit, even if he do be over there fucking with Tootie.

Besides she smoke dope, she don't mess with that other shit as far as he knew. Desmond decided to let DJ sleep it off and try talking to him later when he was cool. Desmond tried calling Shelly to make sure they were good, but she didn't answer. Desmond knew LOC was tired but he asked him to take him to the crib for a while to check on the kids because his sister didn't answer the phone. Just in case Dre showed up and she was scared to answer the phone while he was there. DJ was still sleep so they didn't bother him to tell him. When Desmond got to the crib the first thing he did was check on the kids they all were sound asleep. As he walked up to his mom room to make sure Dre wasn't there he could hear his mom moaning as if she was in there fucking. Desmond turned around and ran down the stairs to go and get the gun DJ had left there that he bought off the streets. He ran back up to his mom's room. He turned the knob to see if her door was unlocked, but she was so busy fucking she didn't hear him. He kicked her bedroom door open and couldn't believe who seen fucking his mother. The one person he looked up to, confided in, and respected the most was in there knocking his mom off. He felt so betrayed. He couldn't believe Dead Eye was fucking his mother.

When they realized Desmond was standing right there. They both jumped up and. Desmond couldn't do anything but shake his head in disbelief. Talonda yelled out "Desmond I'm so sorry baby!" "I never meant to hurt you!" Dead Eye got up and started to get dressed. He walked passed Desmond and said, "be cool lil nigga!" "It's only pussy!" Although Desmond was strapped he couldn't bring his self to put a hole in Dead Eye. He wanted to kick his ass though but he knew he couldn't beat him. At that very moment Desmond was starting to feel like everybody was really against him. He didn't know who he could trust at that moment. He thought about when Shelly told him Dre and his mom got into about her fucking another nigga and it was probably Dead Eye he was talking about the entire time. Desmond knew he couldn't take it to LOC because Dead Eye was his nephew and they were very close.

He even started to think LOC knew about it the entire time, but wasn't saying shit, because that was like a form of dry snitching. Desmond was hurt and distraught he went to Shelly's room and laid on the floor by her bed. When she woke up to use the bathroom she saw Desmond laying on her floor he wasn't sleep but she could tell something was wrong. She went and made him a glass of warm milk to see if that would help. Their grandmother use to give them warm milk to help them sleep when they couldn't sleep. Desmond really ain't want no milk but he took a sip of it because Shelly took the time to make it for him. She asked Desmond if everything was ok. He told yeah everything will be fine just get you sum sleep. I'll stay here tonight so you don't have to worry about anything. Shelly did feel a lot better having her brother there. She felt protected. Desmond had so much anger built up in him, that if Dre walked through that door, he would definitely take his last breath. Dre never showed up and that was a good thing for him, because he didn't have no idea he was going to meet his maker that day. It was a little relief off Desmond's chest.

When the morning hit Desmond got up fixed the kids some breakfast, and tried to get a level head before he took his anger out on everybody. Talonda came down stairs to get something to drink while Desmond was in the kitchen. She told him good morning but he didn't respond. She figured he wouldn't, but she thought he would have gotten over it just a lil bit. Well enough to at least say good morning to her. She sat at the table thinking Desmond had made enough breakfast for her also but he didn't. Talonda apologized to Desmond once again but he wasn't trying to hear shit she was saying. She was pleading for Desmond to forgive her. She tried to give him a hug but he snatched away from her and told her not to fucking hug him. Talonda's mouth dropped she couldn't believe

Desmond had just cursed at her. None of her kids had ever disrespected her. She said in a very hurtful tone, "I know you mad at me Des and I am so fucking sorry!" "I know I been fucking up a lot lately!" "I am human and we all make mistakes!" "I don't know what I would do if I lose my kids, yall all I got!" Desmond said "you should of thought about all that when you turned yo back on yo kids!" "You the reason why Moma Tanya and Auntie Tracy don't come around anymore!" Talonda said "NO!" "They don't come over anymore because they don't want too!" "I never told them they couldn't come over here anymore!"

Desmond said, "Every time they came to check on us and to see what was going on with you, you always found a reason to pick an argument with them." "Talonda said "It was only because they was talking about shit they knew nothing about!" Desmond said to his mom "they only intervened because we called them hungry cuz it was no food!" "Or because you wouldn't get up to cook shit!" Talonda said in a high tone "Des stop cursing at me!" "I'm still your mother!" Desmond looked at his mom and said "well where was you when that nigga Dre was molesting yo fucking daughters!" She responded very sharply "what do you mean Dre was molesting them!" "They never said anything to me about that!" Desmond said "maybe because you was always in yo fucking room sleep or high!" "You right in the house with them and yo punk ass nigga was fucking with yo daughters and you couldn't see that!" "You supposed to be a mother!" "You should know when something wasn't right with your kids!" "Kelley wasn't even eating, her whole damn demeanor changed!" "We noticed something was wrong how come the fuck you didn't!" "We didn't know it was that, "but we knew it was something!" She dropped to her knees and started crying saying to herself "why didn't they tell me?" "I would have protected them!"

Desmond said "you saying that shit now but it's too late!" "The damage has been done!" "The thing is how is you gone repair it?" Talonda was speechless. Desmond said "mom did you ever think about what you were doing to us?" "Everything changed when you started fucking around with him." She didn't even notice Desmond was still cursing at her, maybe because she knew where all his anger was coming from. She started to realize only fucking with Dead Eye just for a free high made shit even worse. Desmond dropped to his knees in front of his mom and looked her in the face and asked her if she was willing to get herself some help so she could be a mother to her kids again. Because they really need her. She knew mentally she wasn't ready because her habit had total control over her but she knew if she told Desmond she wasn't ready it would make everything even worse. Desmond told his mom he loved her no matter what and he wanted his old mom back. "Mom we need you!" "Did you even notice how we were still able to live here and how the bills were getting paid?" Yelled out Desmond. She told Desmond she honestly didn't think about any of that.

Desmond told her the truth because he wanted her to be truthful with him. He told her that he and DJ started selling dope for Dead Eye's and LOC so they could make a living and to keep them from going to foster care and possible getting split up. Talonda was so apologetic that was all she was able to do because she knew everything Desmond was saying was the truth. Desmond told her they will talk later he was about to get into the shower because he had some moves to make. She sat on the floor thinking to herself. As Desmond reach the top stair he heard a loud cry come from his mother. He wanted so bad to go and grab her and hug her, but he knew she needed tough love. Talonda sat on the floor for 15 more minutes she knew her life was in a turmoil. She knew she needed to get help but she didn't know how. After Desmond showered. She called him back into the kitchen and told him she wanted to get some help for herself. She needed to do what was right because she failed her kids. Desmond said, "I don't want you to just say you want help just because everything is fucked up, but because you serious and you need it!" He told her to think long and hard about what she wanted to do and they will go from there.

Talonda looked at Desmond directly in his eyes and told him "everything is about to change!" "Dead Eye won't be coming back over and Dre sorry ass will never step foot through this door ever again". Desmond replied before walking out the door "yeah I hear you!" "I'll believe it when I see you trying!" Before closing the door he yelled to Shelly and said he'll be back to call him if she needed him. Shelley replied, "Will do, and I love you bro, be safe!" Shelly barely told her brothers she loved them. That made Desmond feel sort of good despite all the bullshit going on. After 5 long months she finally called her mom and told her she needed to talk to her. Her mom was happy to hear from her since it's been awhile. She told Talonda she would be right over, Moma Tanya could hear it in Talonda's voice that something was wrong she just didn't know what. Talonda got in the shower and put on some decent clothes she even did her hair and makeup like she use too.

For once she felt so good and confident about herself. When her mother arrived she was shocked to see Talonda all dolled up. She hadn't seen her fix herself up in a couple years. She looked at Talonda and asked her if everything was ok. Talonda looked at her mom with tears in her eyes and said, "no mom it isn't." She started off apologizing for her behavior and how she been acting toward her. He mom accepted her apology. Talonda went on to tell her mom about her drug addiction and told her she needed to get help for herself. He mom agreed. Talonda said, "Mom I'm so hurt!" "I failed my kids miserably and I just found out today that Dre has been molesting my daughters!" Moma Tanya yelled "he did what!" Talonda said "yes mom Des told me today." Moma Tanya asked Talonda where was Desmond and DJ. Talonda said she hasn't seen DJ today actually she didn't know when was the last time she had seen DJ but she didn't tell her mom that. Moma Tanya was furious, she blurted out, "I could kill that bastard!" Talonda has never heard her mom use such language so she knew she was pissed. Moma Tanya asked Talonda if she had spoken with the girls but she told her no she was too embarrassed to face them.

Moma Tanya told Talonda "well you need to overcome that fear and talk to them!" "NOW"! Moma Tanya called the girls into the living room and told them to have a seat. Shelly was almost certain she knew what it was about. Moma Tanya hugged all three girls and told them how much she loved them. When Talonda went to hug them, Moma Tanya saw the separation they had given their mom. Moma Tanya asked the girls one at a time to tell her what happened. The youngest two wouldn't say too much, but Shelly told her grandmother everything that occurred. Moma Tanya told Talonda to get all the kids so they can take the girls to the police station so they could file charges against Dre. Once they arrived at the police station and filed and report they was sent to the hospital to get the girls checked out. Shelly felt like her dignity was being taking from her again, but she knew she had to cooperate. All the girls were checked out and there test showed that had in fact been molested. Shelly tested positive for Chlamydia in her virginal area, and Kelley and Destiny tested positive for having Gonorrhea in the mouth and Chlamydia in the vaginal area. Neither child understood what any of that meant. Child Protective Services was contacted and they gave Talonda a prescription for the girl's sexually transmitted diseases.

Moma Tanya told Talonda while they were there she needed to get herself checked out too. While Moma Tanya sat out in the lobby with the girls Talonda had them to check her also. Talonda tested positive for STD's also. Once they did a thorough pap on her they noticed she had lesions on the inside of her vagina that looked like herpes. Neither one of the girls had herpes but Talonda did. She had no clue she even had neither disease because she had no symptoms. She thought the burning sensation was probably a UTI. It was from the gonorrhea and Herpes, but she didn't know it. She was so prone to getting UTI's because she barely drunk water. The nurse told her sometimes you wouldn't know about the herpes especially if the lesions are on the inside because the virus grow in warm areas.

Eventually it would have spread around the vulva area and you would have encountered some vaginal pain. Talonda knew she had just had been having unprotected sex with Dead Eye also. Since she had what the girls had she knew that came from Dre. So she was thinking she could have gotten herpes from Dead Eye. She was scared to say anything because she wasn't really sure how she encountered the virus. She knew she gave Dead Eye two sexually transmitted diseases and he didn't have a clue. Herpes was something she would have to live with for the rest of her life. She felt like her life was even more in an uproar. The nurse told her she could have come in contact with it sometime awhile back and didn't know it. But she needed to talk to whomever her sexual partners were to find out if any of them had it. She started to think that she may have gotten it from her youngest baby daddy. She was thinking so hard but she still didn't know who could have given it to her.

She knew she needed to tell her mom although she didn't want too. Once she was treated and released with a prescription also. They left the hospital and Moma Tanya took them to get something to eat. At the restaurant Talonda told her mom she wanted to go into a rehab to get herself clean so she can get back on track and be there for her kids. Moma Tanya was willing to do whatever to help her daughter. No matter how old she was that was still her baby. Moma Tanya told Talonda once they got back to her house she would make some calls and get the ball rolling. It would actually help her out a whole lot especially with CPS being contacted about the girls getting molested.

Chapter 6

After leaving the house Desmond called DJ once again. Tootie answered his phone and told Desmond that DJ was in the shower. Desmond told Tootie, "as soon he gets out have him to call me." "ASAP!" "Tell him I'm not fucking playing!" Tootie replied, "yes Des will do." Tootie deleted Desmond's number out the phone and never told DJ to call him. She knew as long as Desmond was in the picture she couldn't control DJ like she wanted too. Whenever DJ was with her he never answered or returned anyone's phone calls unless it was about money. As Desmond left walking to the spot he decided to call LOC to meet him halfway. Once LOC scooped him up he was procrastinating on if he wanted to mention the situation about Dead Eye and his mom. It was fucking with him mentally, but he had to think of a way to approach the situation.

He asked LOC if he had spoken to Dead Eye.

LOC replied "naw nigga!" "I told you when that nigga laying up with them bitches don't think about shit else." Desmond shook his head and told LOC "man I really need to holla at you about some shit that aspired with Dead Eye." "This shit fucked me up when I caught the shit." LOC responded anxiously, "What?" "What's up?" "What you catch?" It took Desmond a few seconds but he turned and looked at LOC and said "remember when you dropped me off at the crib last night?" LOC shook his head forward. Desmond replied "Dog you know I caught that nigga Dead Eye fucking my moma!" LOC look at Desmond with a blank stare and spatted "what the fuck you just say?" Desmond nodded his head forward and replied, "yeah man!" "I did!" "Then the nigga put on his clothes and walked passed me like it was nothing and left." LOC was tripping because he really couldn't believe the shit, but at the same time he could. He knew niggas wasn't loyal. Not even his own nephew.

It sorted pissed LOC off because he knew how DJ and Desmond looked up to him. The more they talked about it the more Desmond was getting pissed all over again. His eyes were starting to fill with water. For once Desmond felt the feeling of being backstabbed. The one person who helped them out and made it possible for them to come out of the slumps done stabbed him in the back. Desmond actually felt the poke in his heart. It fucked LOC up to hear that shit too. Desmond thought LOC wouldn't care because Dead Eye was his nephew and they were very close but LOC actually didn't appreciate the shit at all. LOC knows firsthand that its levels to respect out there in the streets. He wanted to handle the situation in a more logical manner. LOC looked at Desmond and said "youngster I know you mad because that's your mom, and I would be too." "When it comes to the streets it supposed to be a respect thing, but no nigga or bitch gone show no love especially when it's some shit they want." "The same motherfuckers that chop it up with you will underhand you." "See I'm old school motherfuckers lost their lives quick over disrespect." "Don't be pissed off because that ain't the only nigga that your moms would probably fuck out here." "It just hurt because it's that nigga." "Imma tell you some real shit, I never wanted to tell you the shit, but yo moms fucks with that dog food and Dead Eye knew the shit." "I think yo moms probably throw that nigga for sum pussy for sum credit or some shit." Desmond looked at LOC and asked, "What the hell is dog food?" LOC kind of grinned at Desmond and said "I see you ain't been on these streets that long." "It's another name for heroin."

Desmond dropped his head low and whispered to his self "damn my moma fucks with heroin." LOC nodded his head and "said yeah man."

"That was her business so I never said anything." "When I first met her, I saw the marks on her arm." "That's how I knew." LOC replied "That nigga Dre got her on that shit." "That's all he fucks with." Desmond never know how much one person could take til everything started crashing down on him. Desmond blurted out "when I see that nigga Dre, imma kill his bitch ass for fucking my momma life up, and for what the fuck he did to my lil sisters!" LOC said "naw youngster yo moms has a mind of her own." "She chose to fuck with that shit!" "She could have said no, but she didn't." "Dre just and old base head nigga looking for a free ride and she gave him one." LOC was making a lot of sense to Desmond about his mom. He felt a lil bit better about that but he was still pissed about his sisters. Desmond knew DJ was on some bullshit so he felt from here on out he was on his own. LOC and Desmond decided to hit a few blocks.

They rode up by the court to kick it with a few niggas and get their minds right. They noticed as they approached the court it was hella police up there. They saw the yellow tape and the meat wagon so they knew somebody got popped off. They parked the car and jumped out to see what was really going on. They were wheeling the body to the coroners van as they approached the scene. They asked a few people if they knew what had happened and one chick in the crowed said, "It was a dope fiend ass nigga named Dre." Desmond bucked his eyes in disbelief because somebody beat him to Dre already. He wanted the satisfaction of putting that nigga to sleep his self. That was a huge weight lifted off his shoulders, knowing he didn't have to worry about that nigga fucking with his sisters. LOC was trying to find out who could've whacked dat nigga, but nobody knew anything. Dre had been in the abandoned building for several days the coroners stated.

They thought he overdosed but he took one to the back of the head. Everybody in the crowd was saying nine times out of ten he owed somebody some money. They wasn't really sure why he was killed though. They were speculating on what could have happened. LOC pulled Desmond off to the side and asked him if he was sure he had nothing to do with that. LOC made sure he looked at Desmond directly in his eyes when he asked him. Desmond said, "hell naw I ain't do it!" "If I did, do you think I would have been stressing about all the bullshit he did to my fam!" Desmond said, "LOC you was the only person that knew I wanted him dead." "I wouldn't lie to you of all people about killing him." Desmond did tell LOC he felt relieved like a motherfucker though, knowing where his ass would be permanently. LOC believed Desmond was telling him the truth. Once the police got to walking through the crowd asking questionings. DJ was pissing Desmond off so much cuz he still wasn't answering his phone. LOC told Desmond to call back and leave a message on DJ's phone. They headed back to the spot to chill hoping DJ would pop up. They haven't heard from him and they were starting to worry if he was cool. Instead Dead Eye came a few hours later. When Dead Eye walked in the crib he looked at Desmond and said very nonchalantly. "I guess you pissed I was putting meat in yo moms."

Desmond started to breathe real fast and his eyes started to fill with water again, but he made sure he held back his tears back, and said with a very smart tone. "I really don't give a shit!" "Her life already fucked up!" He really didn't feel that way, he knew he couldn't whoop Dead Eye's ass though. LOC spoke up and told Dead Eye he was real foul for that shit. Dead Eye responded with a smurk on his face as if he didn't give a shit. "Yeah I know!" "She had sum good pussy though!" Dead Eye held out his fist to give Desmond some Daps. Desmond didn't want to dap his fist but he did it anyways. As Dead Eye walked off he said to Desmond, "nigga it's a cold game out here!" "Don't nobody play fair nomo!" At that very moment Desmond knew he couldn't trust Dead Eye on shit no more. Desmond had so much on is mind he couldn't seem to gather his thoughts. One thing he knew for damn sho was that he had to be a movement by his damn self. He didn't want to cut DJ all the way off, but he felt like DJ been cut him off. Desmond couldn't get how DJ let Tootie fuck his head up.

Desmond knew that wasn't his first piece of pussy. They lost their virginity the same night. Desmond started to think back like damn was this nigga fucking my moma when he did all that shit for us. Maybe he started fucking my moma after they came over for the Christmas holiday. Desmond didn't know when they started fucking, all he knew was he caught them. DJ was acting like Tootie was his bitch or something by the way he be up under her so much. Even as a younger child DJ knew Tootie use to gank niggas for money. She used to get the shit beat out her ass back in the day for ganking niggas. Now that Dre was out of the way, Desmond felt like he had to worry about Dead Eye or any other niggas his moma felt like she wanted to trick off with. After what Dre did he didn't want no other niggas around his lil sisters. Desmond had so many thoughts flowing through his head he just wanted to go home and get himself together. Desmond asked LOC to drop him off at the crib. While they were in the car it was complete silence. LOC knew Desmond had a lot on his mind.

When they pulled up at Desmond's crib as he began to exit the car. LOC looked at Desmond and said, "younsta I know what you thinking about doing and don't go out here and do no stupid shit!" "I'm leaving you at the crib so keep yo ass here!" "Call me if you need me!" LOC was pretty much the only person that hadn't turned on him. Desmond was starting to regret the lifestyle he and DJ chose. He thought that no matter what him and DJ would remain close and always be there for each other. Instead DJ was starting to let all that bullshit go to his head. He starting seeing money he never thought he would see at that age. He was fucking some of the baddest bitches around. Some older niggas dreamed of fucking the type of bitches DJ was pulling. DJ was always mobile because either Tootie rented him a luxury car in her name. Or it was always somebody looking to get a quick fix. DJ was turning into a real cold-hearted ass nigga. Desmond always had love for Tootie after all she was their godmother. For some odd reason he had a gut feeling she was a part of the problem.

Talonda was going to go into a treatment program so that meant they were gonna have to go stay at their grandmother's. Unless DJ get his act together. He was damn near 18 so it shouldn't be that big of problem. All Desmond knew was if DJ didn't get with him so they could think of a plan they would both be missing out on money. Living at their grandmother's house would be real fucked up for them. They would have to use all the money that was saved. Desmond didn't know if DJ still had money saved or not. All Desmond had saved up was about nine racks and he knew the bills in the house would take all of that in no time. Desmond kept calling DJ but it went straight to voicemail. So he said fuck it he asked his mother will they be able to stay at home if their Auntie Tracey came to check on them. Moma Tanya didn't like that idea at all she felt like the kids should come to her house. Desmond said "but if no one is at our house we are pretty much inviting people to break in." Moma Tanya said "I will come by and check on the house daily." DJ looked at his granny, shook his head and said, "Granny we live in the hood, people will see you coming and going all the time." He caught Moma Tanya by surprise because he never calls her granny.

Talonda looked at her mom and said, "He does have a point mom." Although Moma Tanya didn't feel comfortable with that idea. She didn't want to give Talonda a reason not to go into Rehab. Moma Tanya looked back at Talonda and said, "Well I guess we will give it a try." "After all they have been keeping the house together while you were going through your ordeal." Desmond knew his mom was already feeling guilty about getting caught with Dead Eye. He knew she would agree with almost anything at that moment. He decided to holla at his moms. First he apologized for cursing at her. He then brought to her attention that the entire time she was off her rockers he and DJ was the reason why the bills was getting paid, and why they still had a roof over their heads. Shelly was making sure the kids were fed and changed and in bed on time. Talonda agreed with everything Desmond was saying.

He told her, "If we did all this while you were getting high what makes you think we can't hold it down while you gone." "Besides I will be around the house more and I promise not to do anything illegal out the crib." All he wanted was for his mom to get the help she needed so she could get back to her old self. She use to be so pretty when she took care of herself. Talonda felt bad because she had already given them so much responsibility that she didn't want to really put no more on them than she had too. Desmond couldn't sugarcoat shit anymore he knew he just had to be straightforward with Talonda from here on out. Although they were storing their dope in her house he didn't want his mom to know so she won't renege on going to rehab. Talonda called to see if the rehab in Kissimmee had any open slots. She wanted to go far away from home hoping she wouldn't see anyone she knew because of embarrassment. Talonda was excited to hear that they had an opening for her. They would also fly a nurse and the social worker out to do a pre assessment on her and fly her back out with them.

Talonda had two days to have her things packed and ready to go when they arrived to pick her up. She sat the table with her mom and drank a glass of tea. She also told her mom that she wanted to free herself from all the demons she's been caring around for so many years. Her mom didn't have a clue that Talonda was bothered by anything. She has always seemed very normal until she met Dre. Moma Tanya looked at Talonda with a blank stare. She trying figure out what demons could Talonda be caring inside of her. All kinds of thoughts was flowing through her mind as she waited on Talonda to gather her thoughts. She didn't know if any of that lead to Talonda's drug usage and why she going through these obstacles in her life. Talonda sat and looked at her mom as tears began to flow down her face. This was harder than her admitting her drug problem to Desmond. Moma Tanya waited anxiously as Talonda began to tell her. Talonda cleared her throat and told her mom that a long time ago when she first separated from their dad and got with the man Bruce he use to force her to have sex with him and force her to have oral sex with him. Moma Talonda didn't want to believe what Talonda was telling her.

She thought Bruce loved her girls because he took good care of them from little kids to they became teenagers. Hearing that was a hard pill for Moma Tanya to swallow. Talonda took a deep swallow of her tea and went on to tell her mom that Bruce was DJ's father. Moma Tanya jumped out her chair and covered her ears crying and yelling "STOP TALONDA!" "STOP!" "I CAN"T HEAR NO MORE OF THIS!" Moma Tanya fell to her knees, then laying on the floor yelling "GOD WHY?!" "WHY YOU LET THIS HAPPEN TO MY DAUGHTER?!" Talonda grabbed her mom and picked her up from the floor and gave her a tight hug and said. "It's okay mom!" "Please stop crying." "I wanted to tell you years ago but I thought you would be mad at me." Moma Tanya held

Talonda by her cheeks and kissed her on her forehead and told her "you didn't have to be scared to tell me anything." "I wouldn't have gotten mad at you." I would've believed you." "Moma Tanya asked Talonda if he had touched Tracey as well. Talonda told her mom, "I did everything he wanted me to do to keep him from touching Tracy." Moma Tanya knew it wasn't anything she could do because of the statute of limitations in their state.

Bruce had passed away a few years ago due to a heart attack. Moma Tanya told Talonda "I wouldn't have never been with a man that was messing with my girls." "All I could think of is the coulda's, woulda's and shoulda's but it won't change what has already happened." Moma Tanya sat there in a daze thinking to herself..... (Now that she said this, DJ do look a lot like Bruce)..... She didn't want to say it out loud in front of Talonda. She wasn't trying to upset her and cause her to change her mind about going to rehab. Moma Tanya grabbed Talonda's hand and began to pray. Asking GOD to remove all the demons and negative people out their family. Moma Tanya knew she couldn't tell Talonda's dad he was already sick and he would be very upset with her. She told Talonda to keep that between them she didn't want it to get out and the kids ending up finding out the truth. Talonda always wanted to tell DJ the truth about who his real father was.

Although he would never get the chance to ever see him. Moma Tanya mumbled under her breath... (I hope you burn in hell you bastard for what you did to my daughter)... Talonda thought to herself... (maybe mom is right by not mentioning anything)... Since she told her mom about the secret she's been carrying for many years. She felt so much better and was ready to go into rehab. Moma Tanya couldn't stop crying but she had to pull herself together before the kids saw her and start to ask questions. Moma Tanya started to feel like she failed her daughter also. She wanted to do whatever she could to make it up to Talonda but it's been almost 20 years since it has happened. Talonda looked at her mom and said, "this is why I never wanted to tell you." "I knew you would beat yourself up over it." Moma Tanya told Talonda she's trying to be strong but it's hurting her so bad on the inside. Talonda was afraid that her mom would be stressing the entire time she's away in rehab. Moma Tanya told Talonda, "I wasn't there to save you or my grandkids and its killing me on the inside." Talonda went to get her mom a washrag to clean her face.

While she was in the restroom she heard a big boom. She ran out the restroom to go and check to see what was going on. Moma Tanya had passed out on the floor and started to vomit. Talonda yelled for the kids to dial 911. The kids ran into the kitchen to see what was going on and Talonda kept yelling for them to call 911. Shelly ran and called 911. Talonda sat on the floor and held her mom til the paramedics arrived. When they arrived Moma Tanya was unresponsive. They hurried and rushed her to the hospital. Talonda called Tracey and told her what happened. Tracey was at the house watching her dad, she didn't tell him what was going on she called next door to the neighbor's house to see if they could watch the house while goes to the hospital to check on her mom. Talonda was ready to go out and get high because she can't handle being under pressure. Getting high became a way out for her. It made her forget about everything that was wrong in her life.

She was itching so bad to go and get high, but she didn't want to let her mom or her kids down. She began to pray in the hospital. She asked GOD to deliver the urge to get high from her. She also asked GOD that if he would put his healing hands on her mom and cover her in his blood. Talonda had two days to go before going to rehab and she didn't want to leave her mom. She knew that if she didn't go when they came she wouldn't be able to go and they wasn't gone take her serious. She paced back and forth in the hospital trying to permit herself from leaving to get one more fix. She started to sweat and something just told her to keep praying for herself and her mom. While she was praying the nurse came in and told Talonda her mom had a stroke and her stress levels was very high. Talonda started to blame herself for her mom having a stroke. She wished she would have just kept everything a secret despite how good it felt to get it out. Tracy arrived at the hospital, Talonda was a little relieved and her urge to go and get high left all of a sudden. Talonda explained to her sister what was going on with their mom. Without telling her about their conversation.

The doctor ran some more test on Moma Tanya and told the girls that she would be getting admitted into the hospital. Talonda knew she would be gone for 180 days in the treatment center. She didn't want to leave her mom's side, but she knew it would make her mom feel a lot better if she went forward with the process. For once in a very long time Talonda wanted to do something right. Shelly called Desmond to tell him what happened to their granny and he rushed up to the hospital as quickly as he could on his bike. He didn't wait for no ride, nor did he try and call DJ. Shelly tried calling DJ but he didn't answer. When Desmond finally arrived at the hospital he was hysterical, he didn't know what was going on. When he went into the emergency room and saw on the tubes and wires his granny was hooked up too. He burst into tears. He thought she had died. He has never seen no one hooked up to tubes and wires before. Talonda and Tracey grabbed Desmond and hugged him telling him granny will be okay. Desmond walked away from them and laid his head on his granny chest telling her he was right there and how much he loved her. She couldn't respond to him because of the tube in her throat and she was unconscious.

All he wanted her to do was respond to him just one time. He grabbed her hand and started rubbing and kissing her hand. He told her he would be right there when she woke up. At least he wanted to be there. He didn't know how long it would take her to wake up. Talonda felt like she was strong enough to stay clean until her mom woke up. She went into the lobby and called the treatment center and explained to them what happened to her mom and they said they would reschedule her. She had to make sure she called them back once her mom was fine. They stayed at the hospital for a few hours. Desmond left to go and find DJ. Tracey dropped Talonda off at home. She knew her dad would be looking for their mom so she was gone tell him she was staying over Talonda's to help her out with the kids. After Tracey dropped Talonda off she started having the cravings to get high again. She tried praying but the cravings and withdrawals was getting the best of her. She decided to take a nap to see if it would reduce her cravings. She woke up a couple hours later. Once she saw the kids were all asleep and Desmond and DJ wasn't home she decided to get dressed and leave. She walked down to the dope house to turn a trick to feed her craving.

Once she walked up to the door and began to knock she caught herself and ran away from the house crying. When she got back home she called for Desmond to come home. She told Desmond she was under pressure and she was getting the urge to go and get high. Desmond told her he was on his way home and not to leave. Talonda sat there and waited for Desmond to come home. When Desmond walked through the door Talonda was in the bathroom running cold water over her face to get rid of the hot flashes and sweats she was getting due to the withdraws. Desmond grabbed his mom and told her how much he loved her and appreciated her despite all she's been through. Talonda never told Desmond the truth about how her mom had the stroke. She did tell Desmond she was trying to be strong that's why she called him. She told him she left to go and try to get high, but she ran back home and called him.

Desmond fixed her a bowl of soup and he stayed with her so she wouldn't leave. Desmond decided to sleep in the bed with his mom to keep an eye on her. It felt awkward because he hadn't did that since he was a kid. The next morning Talonda fixed her and the kids sum breakfast. She got dressed and waited for Tracey to take her up to the hospital. Desmond had already left the house. When they arrived at the hospital Desmond was already there holding his granny's hand and talking to her. When Talonda and Tracey heard her responding to Desmond they felt a sense of relief and happy at the same time. Talonda thanked GOD for removing the urge of her wanting to get high and bringing her mom back to consciousness. Moma Tanya looked at Talonda and smiled as if she was her Guardian Angel. At that very moment Talonda realized that she had the power to concur her addiction. She refused to let it get the best of her.

She didn't bring up anything about the treatment center or their previous conversations she just sat there and talked to her mom about happy things. Tracey was so busy kissing her mom and telling her how much she loved her. Once Talonda got the help she needed she could return and focus on building a better relationship with her kids and family again. Talonda walked out into the hallway and called the treatment center and asked them what was the earliest they could come to get her, because her mom had awakened and she on the road to recovery and she wanted to be on the road to recovery also. They could hear the seriousness in Talonda's voice they told her they could be there in 72 hours to assess her and bring her to start her treatment. Talonda accepted the offer. She didn't want to tell her mom, but she told Tracey and Desmond what her plans were and not to tell Moma Tanya just let her get better. Tracey was excited for her sister. It was well over due. Desmond was very happy for his mom. Tracey told Desmond they gone have to work as a team taking care of grandma, granddaddy and the kids. Desmond told his aunt Tracey to focus on his grandparents he would make sure the kids was straight. Talonda couldn't believe how mature Desmond had become.

Tracey even noticed how mature Desmond was. Tracey asked Desmond where was DJ, and he didn't have a clue. He didn't want to say he hadn't talked to him so he told her he hadn't talked to him since earlier that morning. Talonda's things were already packed so she spent the next couple days at the hospital and with her kids. Talonda was actually proud of herself for once in a very long time. She knew she was doing the right thing for herself and her family. When Talonda returned home after leaving the hospital. She cooked dinner for her and the kids; they all sat and ate together like a family minus Desmond because he stayed at the hospital, and DJ because he was out running the streets. They all watched the comedy channel together and laughed until everyone had gotten tired and went to bed. Talonda sat up and washed the dishes and waited for her older two to come in. Desmond was the only one who showed up. Talonda told him that him and DJ's plate was in the oven if they were hungry. Talonda asked Desmond where do DJ be at and why he's never home. She was starting to think DJ was locked up and Desmond was covering for him.

Desmond told her he was down the street playing the game with his friend. Talonda didn't believe him she called all the jails and hospitals to see if he was there but there was no D'wayne Thompson listed in their records with his date of birth. Desmond said mom why are you calling all those places I told you he's at his friend's house. Talonda called DJ's phone and he answered finally. She asked DJ where was he at and he said out with his friends. She told DJ that Moma Tanya was in the hospital and asked why he hadn't been to see her. DJ asked his mom what was wrong with granny and Talonda told him she had a stroke. DJ felt like shit knowing his granny had been in the hospital for two days and he didn't know it. He told his mom he will go up there tomorrow to see his granny and he would be home in a few. Once DJ hung up from his mom he texted Desmond and cursed him out for not letting him know what was going on. Desmond texted DJ back and told him if you would answer yo fucking phone you would know about everything that's been going on. Desmond told DJ he needed to come like ASAP so he could let him know about everything and their mom would be leaving in 24 hours and he needed to see her before she had left. Desmond sat up damn near all night waiting for DJ and he never showed up.

Chapter 7

W hen the day came for Talonda to report to rehab she started having mixed emotions about going. Desmond was still pissed about his sisters getting molested and he blamed his mom for it but didn't let her know he did. Talonda knew a lot of the things that went on was her fault. If she wasn't getting high and fucking with Dre she woulda been able to protect her babies. Talonda went to see her mom for a few hours and spend the rest of her time with her kids before they came to get her at 4pm. She called DJ's phone over and over but he didn't answer. Desmond told her not to worry DJ was fine and he will make sure he calls her if she doesn't get the chance to see him before they came to get her. Talonda kept hugging and kissing her children as the time got closer for her to leave. She started to cry because she was going to miss her babies but she had to do what was right. When 3:30pm hit.

They arrived to assess Talonda and prepare for her departure. The nurse checked her out and made sure she was in her right state of mind. She asked her a series of questions as they taped the conversation so Talonda couldn't say she was forced to go into rehabilitation and she was going on her own free will. Once the assessment process was over Talonda prepared herself to leave. DJ still hadn't showed up. She started to cry and the kids started to cry as well. They weren't use to being home without their mom being totally gone. Regardless of how she mistreated them during her drug addiction. She kissed her babies goodbye and she was ready to begin her journey to recovery. Once Talonda made it to the center, she had to go through the listing process and get registered. After the registration process she had a series of meetings to attend so she can get acquainted with the others that was in rehab as well. She was new to everything so she stayed quiet during the meetings and sat back and listened to the other's talk about their problems. When she was asked to if she had anything she wanted to say she nodded her head no.

They didn't pressure her because it was her first day in the facility. As the days passed Talonda started getting used to being there she tried not to worry about her mom and kids and focus so she wouldn't be stressing herself. Although she couldn't talk to her family for 30 days she made sure she stayed strong. Desmond and the other kids wrote her weekly and sent her photos. He thought that would make her very happy. Deep down on the inside it crushed her soul. She missed out on so much with her kids. The youngest Devin had started getting potty-trained and was about to turn 2. Donald was about to turn 4. Shelly taught him his alphabets and numbers. Destiny is gradually coming back to her old self again. Kelley is getting bigger but she's still shy. Aseanti would be turning 8 after Talonda completes to the program. Talonda couldn't do anything until she gotten herself all the way together. Desmond never told his mom that Dre had been killed and he wasn't going to tell her. Desmond and the kids continued to write their mom and send updated photos to her. It started to make her feel good knowing they didn't give up on her like she did them. She heard from everybody accept for DJ. She didn't let that discourage her. She was able sit in meetings and discuss her problems and issues instead of just listening to everyone else's problems. She met people that had similar situations as hers. Talonda was starting to find herself in a good place in her life. She hadn't felt that good in 30 days needless to say. Her body was starting to feel pure.

Since she was doing so good with the program the case manager allowed her to call her children and her mom talk to them for an hour since she had 7 children. Talking to her kids on the phone made her so happy and it gave her the encouragement to keep going and not give up. Desmond was taking care of the house as planned. Her mom was released from the hospital two weeks after she was admitted. Talonda asked Desmond to speak to DJ but as usual he was not around. She asked Desmond why haven't DJ wrote her or sent her any pictures. Desmond didn't want to upset her. He told her, "DJ got himself a girlfriend and now he's smelling himself." Talonda laughed and said "wow my babies are finally growing into young men." She told Desmond, "I hope neither one of yall make me a grandmother no time soon." Desmond laughed and said "naw ma we not on that right now at least I'm not." Talonda told Desmond, "I really appreciates you for stepping up and becoming the man of the house." "While I'm gone and DJ is never there anymore." Aunt Tracey comes by to check on the kids daily and calls throughout the day. Talonda had to end her phone conversation because she had a meeting to attend. She told her mom she loved her and her dad.

She told her sister as well. Once she ended the phone call she cried tears of joy. For once she was very proud of herself. School will be starting before Talonda completes her treatment. Tracey will see to it that the older kids are straight and squared away for school. Moma Tanya was getting well enough to look after Devin because he was too young for preschool. Once Talonda knew everything was handled at home. She focused on herself. Desmond tried calling DJ he finally answered and Desmond snapped on him. He asked DJ "what the fuck is your problem!" DJ responded, "what you mean bro?" Desmond told him, "You don't answer any of my texts or phone calls!" DJ responded to Desmond, "it ain't like you wanted shit!" Desmond then got pissed off. He demanded DJ to bring his ass to the crib because we needed to talk ASAP. He told DJ, "drop whatever bitch you with off or whomever you with and come home!" DJ told Desmond, "I'm by myself." Desmond responded, "oh that's why you answered huh!" "Man just bring yo ass to the crib so we can holla!" stated Desmond. Desmond stayed at the crib waiting for DJ to come that he ended up dozing off and waking up two hours later. DJ still hadn't showed up yet. He called DJ's phone and it went straight to voicemail. He called LOC to see if he heard from DJ. He hadn't heard from DJ ever since they all was at the spot together the night he was tripping.

Desmond was fed up with DJ's shit. He wasn't gone call him no more. He was about to be on his own shit. Desmond got dressed and decided to walk around through the hood and try to make as much as he could. So he can get all the shit they needed for school. He didn't know if DJ was gone go back to school or not. He didn't want to be in the dope game for the rest of his life he want to become something in life. Everybody was so used to seeing the brothers together they were all shocked to see Desmond walking through the hood by his self. Desmond decided to chill up on Palmer Rd. he could make a lil more of his money up there, especially if nobody else was up there. After he made him a good $400 he went to the crib to put that shit up. He jumped on his old bike and road around to see if he could make a lil mo bread before it got too late. It was a lil dry out he made another quick $60 and went back to the crib for the night. He asked Shelly when he got in if DJ ever showed up and she responded, "No!" Desmond shook his head and laid across the couch while the kids were playing with their toys. Shelly went and sat on the porch for a while. Desmond wasn't gone leave the kids at home by themselves to long. He knew DJ kept a strap at the crib so he was really tripping off no bulllshit.

He knew eventually he was gone have to get his own strap in case DJ decided to ever come and get his. While Desmond was chilling his phone ranged. He didn't recognize the number so he didn't answer. They called back so he decided to answer in case something was wrong with DJ. It was a female asking for Desmond. The voice was unfamiliar to him. Instantly he got butterflies in his stomach. Thinking somebody was calling him to tell him something about DJ. Females didn't call his phone unless they was trying do business with him. That voice sounded a lil too young for them to be getting high. That wasn't the case though. It was ol' girl Krystal that lived a couple blocks down from them. He was surprised that she would call him out of the blu like that. He was even more surprised that she had his number. Krystal was fine as hell to Desmond. He didn't even think to ask her how she gotten his number.

Krystal was about 5Ft even and thick as shit. Desmond always thought she was cute, but she never said two words to him. Krystal told Desmond she got the number from a friend. He didn't care who the friend was he was happy she called him. He hollered at her for about 5 more minutes, then told her he will call her back. Once they hung up he started to wonder how she could've gotten his number. He don't really fuck with nobody in the hood like that. He barely saw her with friends even when they was in school. He couldn't put two and two together so he said fuck it. He had bigger shit to stress over. He sat and watched TV for a while. Shelly came in from outside and started getting the kids ready for bed. A few hours later Shelly came downstairs to cut the TV off thinking Desmond was asleep on the couch. Desmond looked over and asked Shelly if she had given out his number to anybody.

She told Desmond she had given it to Krystal from down the street because she liked him. That took a load off his shoulders. He was beginning to think a motherfucker was trying to set him up or sum shit. Shelly told Desmond while she was outside letting the kids play. Krystal was on her way to the candy store and she sat with her and the kids for a while until they were done playing. Krystal had told her that she had a crush on Desmond but she was scared that he wouldn't be interested in her. So she gave her the number and told her to call him. Desmond was gone call her back but it had gotten late and he wanted to be respectable. He went on and crashed out for the night and was gone hit her up in the morning. Shelly ended up falling asleep on the love seat. Around 4:30 in the morning Desmond woke up to Shelly screaming, swinging and kicking as if she was fighting somebody off f her. Desmond jumped up off the couch and woke her up. She started to cry and was hugging Desmond fairly tight telling him that she has nightmares like Dre was still hurting her. Desmond knew Dre was dead but he didn't want to tell his sister. Then again it might have made her feel better knowing. Desmond couldn't wait for his mom to come back because they needed help bad. He knew she had to help herself before she could begin to help them.

Desmond had no clue his mother had endured the same sexual abuse as his sisters. The only difference was she conceived a child during her abuse. Desmond told Shelly to try and get some rest he would lay in the floor next to the couch and make sure nobody harms her. For some odd reason she wouldn't stop crying. Desmond told her everything was okay. She looked at Desmond and said no it's not. Desmond told her Dre is gone he is not coming back. She looked at him and told him Dre was not the only person hurting her. Desmond rose his head up and said "what the fuck you mean Dre isn't the only one!" Before she could respond Desmond thought Dead Eye's had been fucking with his sister too. Shelley looked at Desmond and said, "Please don't be mad at me Des." Desmond responded as calmly as he could. "I'm not gone be mad at you Shelly." She told Desmond that about a couple of weeks ago DJ came to the house and made her suck his private. Desmond jumped off the floor and grabbed her by her shoulders, but not intentionally to hurt or scare her. She went on to tell him that when DJ came home he was acting real weird and calling her some other girl's name. Then he started unzipping his pants and forcing her head down by his private area. She said he was getting real aggressive with her.

He starting hitting her and calling bitches and telling her she better give him sum head. She kept asking him what was he doing and he grabbed her and said bitch you better suck this dick. She told Desmond she was so scared because he kept on hitting her so she went on and did it so he would leave her alone. She said she was screaming for their mom but she was in a deep sleep. Desmond had fire in his eyes he instantly got pissed at his mom again because she was so high she couldn't hear her own daughter screaming for her to come save her. He was even more pissed at DJ. At that very moment Desmond knew him and DJ's relationship was over. Desmond wanted to leave and ride around the city on his bike looking for DJ. He knew he couldn't leave Shelly alone with the kids because she was already terrified. Once Shelly went to sleep after Desmond calmed her down and told her from that point on he wouldn't let nobody else hurt her or his lil sisters ever again including DJ.

Desmond was pass his breaking point. He couldn't take it no more he broke down and started crying. He didn't want to wake Shelly but he was so pissed that all he could do was cry. He didn't want to tell LOC because it was a family matter. He couldn't tell his mom. He didn't want her to relapse. He couldn't tell his aunt Tracey because she tells their granny everything. This was something he had to deal with on his own. The following morning Desmond was still awake he couldn't even sleep after Shelly told him what DJ had done. Krystal called him and talking to a bitch was the last thing on his mind. Every little thing was pissing him off. He didn't have an appetite or nothing. His main focus was to find DJ. He knew DJ wouldn't answer his phone calls so he had one of their hypes to call DJ's phone like they were trying to get something but he didn't answer. As Desmond was about to ride off DJ called back and he had the hype tell DJ he wanted him to meet him somewhere. DJ asked where. Desmond told the hype to tell DJ by the corner store.

About 30 minutes later DJ pulled up and he was by himself. Desmond ran up on DJ and socked him in the mouth while he was sitting in the car. DJ jumped out the car and swung on Desmond and they started fighting a lil ways down from the corner store. While they were out there LOC was riding pass and saw them out there fighting and tried to break it up. Although Desmond was younger than DJ he was beating his ass. DJ broke away from Desmond and ran to the car and got his gun and started shooting at Desmond, he hid behind a car to avoid getting shot. Luckily he missed. LOC jumped from his car and was trying to wrestle the gun from DJ. When he dropped the gun Desmond ran and picked it up and shot DJ twice in the chest. LOC ran over and grabbed Desmond and took the gun from him. Desmond stumbled back trying to catch his balance. He was in total shock at that moment. He didn't know if he had shot DJ or not. The loud pop from the gun scared him so bad, he got nervous. Everything was complete silence after the second pop. Everyone was moving in slow motion. Gradually the sound of screaming was coming back to his ears.

He then realized that DJ was bleeding from his chest. As he looked around he saw everybody screaming and yelling. LOC ran back over to DJ to see is he was cool he told Desmond to ride off before the police came. While they were waiting for the ambulance to come DJ took his last breath in LOC's arms. LOC had one of his hypes to walk off with the gun. Desmond road off but he was paranoid from what had just happened. He was riding around on his bike but didn't know where he was riding too. He was in total shock, everything happened so fast. He didn't know that his brother died. He didn't have nobody he could talk too about what had just happened. He rode his bike 10 miles away from their area. He couldn't succumb the tragedy. He tried calling LOC but his fingers was dialing the wrong number because he was so nervous. He had to wait until his adrenaline calmed down, so he could call LOC.

When he finally called LOC's phone. LOC answered as if Desmond was a female and said babe imma have to call you back I'm talking to the police right now. Desmond hung up very quickly. The only person left was his aunt Tracey. He called her and told her the street he was on and what he was by so she could come to him. He didn't tell her what happened but she could hear in his voice that it was something serious. Tracey grabbed her purse and ran out the car driving as fast as she could to Desmond trying not to get pulled over for speeding. When Tracey arrived to where Desmond was. She saw Desmond sitting by a tree crying. She jumped out the car and ran over to him asking forcefully what was wrong. Desmond hugged her very tight and said "I didn't mean to do it!" "I didn't mean too I swear!" Tracey asked Desmond, "What did you do?" Desmond couldn't stop crying to tell Tracey what he had done. Tracey wiped the running tears from his face and sat on the ground next to him. She kept telling Desmond to talk to her. Tell her what was going on.

Desmond asked her if she could go across the street and get him another bottle water. His mouth was getting dry again. Tracey went and got Desmond another bottle water so he could calm down and talk to her. Desmond was starting to calm down enough to tell Tracey what happened from the beginning when Shelly told him what DJ had done to her, and what lead up to him shooting DJ in the chest twice. Neither one knew that DJ died at the scene. Tracy told Desmond to put his bike car in her truck so she could take him home. Desmond didn't want to go home he knew the police would be looking for him there. Tracey went and rented a hotel room for Desmond until she went to see what was going on with DJ. When Tracy arrived at the scene she saw so many police and detectives. DJ was still laying on the ground uncovered. She saw LOC standing there with blood all over him. She ran over the crime scene tape yelling and screaming. "GOD NO!" "PLEASE TELL ME THAT'S NOT MY NEPHEW!"

She kept yelling for DJ to get up, but there wasn't any movement from DJ. He was laying on the ground as if he was asleep. One of the detectives came over to Tracey to get information about DJ because he had no ID on him. She asked the Detective what happened to her nephew. The Detective was asking Tracey if she knew or heard anything. They didn't have any leads at the moment. None of the witness would come forward. Tracey knew she couldn't harbor Desmond for killing DJ. They both were her nephews. She was completely lost on what to do. She felt like that was the biggest decision she ever had to make. She didn't know if she wanted to turn her nephew in for killing her other nephew whom was his brother. Talonda was away and her mom was still sick. She sat at the scene until DJ's body was carried away. She went back to the hotel to get the full story from Desmond again.

She couldn't quite get what he was saying. She decided to go and talk to Shelly herself. While Tracey was on her way to talk to Shelly. Desmond sat there pacing back and forth in the hotel thinking about what to do. LOC called him back. He answered the phone on the first ring. LOC told him so far the police don't know who did it. LOC had to ask Desmond what provoked him to kill his brother. Desmond told LOC about what Shelly told him also. He also told him that his aunt Tracey was on her way over there to talk to his sister. LOC was fucked up behind that conversation. He knew DJ stayed on bullshit but he never thought he would do some fucked up shit like that. For a moment LOC felt like DJ got what he deserved for doing that shit. It was just a fucked up situation because it was his own brother who took his life. Desmond knew he couldn't stay on the run for too much longer. Eventually it was gone come out. He just didn't know when and who would tell it.

When Tracy got to Talonda's house she sat down with Shelly and discuss the DJ situation with her and Shelly repeated everything she had told Desmond. She even told Tracey about what Dre had done to her and her sisters. The more Tracey heard the more of a fucked up situation she was in. She knew eventually she was gone have to tell her mom and notify Talonda. LOC told Desmond to lay low for a while until everything calms down. On the other hand Tracey knew she couldn't withhold any information from her mom and Talonda. After talking to Shelley she didn't tell her that DJ was dead. She went back to the hotel to make sure Desmond as okay. After sitting up there talking to Desmond for a while she convinced him to turn himself in. Desmond was terrified of jail he was only sixteen. He hadn't never been to jail before. He did know he could be charged as an adult and go to prison for the rest of his life. Desmond asked Tracey if she would give him a couple of days before he turned himself in. In the meantime Tracey had to find a way to break the news to her family. She called Talonda's case manager first so they could tell Talonda. An hour later Talonda called Tracey to see what was going on.

She didn't tell her that Desmond did it because she didn't know if they taped Talonda's conversation. If nothing else made Talonda relapse Tracey knew that would. The counselor's and case manager talked to Talonda before she was sent back to society about how important it was for her to be strong and staying clean. Talonda only completed a month and a half of her sobriety. That wasn't enough time for her to get properly clean. Losing a child is a hard pill to swallow. Especially for a parent that didn't get to see or speak to their child before they died. The counselor found a center in Talonda's home town so they could support her through this difficult time for her. They would continue to work with Talonda also. They knew she was serious about getting herself cleaned and working toward being a better parent to her kids. Talonda blamed herself once again. Her case manager decided to be there and help Talonda with resources so she could get help with DJ's burial. Once Tracey talked to Talonda and got that out of the way. She knew she had to tell her mom. She decided to wait til Talonda made it home before she mentioned it. Tracey also decided to let Desmond stay out so he could attend DJ's funeral. Tracey went and stayed over Talonda's house because she knew the police and detectives would be coming over. None of the police mentioned Desmond's name so Tracey knew he wasn't a suspect. 24 hours later Talonda arrived home. Tracy was there with the kids.

Desmond was not there. Talonda asked Tracey where was Desmond. Tracey told Talonda to have a seat so they can talk. Tracey told her everything that lead up to DJ's murder including what Shelly told her. Talonda dropped her head and started crying. She mumbled to herself in a low voice. DJ was just like his daddy and I never paid any attention. Tracy told Talonda you can't blame his daddy for DJ's actions. Talonda told Tracy DJ's daddy molested her just like DJ did Shelly the difference was it was their mom's old boyfriend Bruce. When she separated from their dad. Tracey said in shock "BRUCE!" "So you saying Bruce is DJ's daddy?" Talonda shook her head and said "yeah." "That's how I had DJ at the age of thirteen." "Even after DJ he was still doing it but I had a boyfriend at the time so I don't know if he's Desmond's father too or the other dude is." Replied Talonda.

Talonda didn't tell her mom that it was a possibility that Bruce could be Desmond's father also. She kind of glad she didn't that would have been more stress on her. Tracey asked Talonda why she didn't never tell. Talonda said she was scared to tell. She told Tracey, "I did whatever he wanted to do to keep him from messing with you." Tracey was in disbelief because Bruce never touched her inappropriately. Talonda told Tracey "that's why I was so happy when mom left Bruce and gotten back with dad." After hearing Talonda's story Tracey told Talonda "I can see why you went down the path you did." "You kept a secret like that for so many years and no one never knew." Talonda told Tracey "I'm not gone use that as an excuse for why I started using drugs because I had choices and I chose to make all the wrong ones." Talonda was so fucked up about her sons the last thing on her mind was getting high. Talonda broke the news to the kids about DJ's death.

Once Shelly heard what happened she walked off. Talonda was gone talk to Shelly in front of Tracey, but she needed to talk to her daughter one on one. Tracey took Talonda up to the hotel so she could see Desmond. When Desmond saw his mom walk into his room. He broke down and cried all over again. He hugged her so tight and told her he was sorry and begged her for forgiveness. He told her he only went to talk to DJ but he had gotten so mad all over again when he seen him. He just hit him and they started fighting. DJ pulled the gun out and shot at him first. When LOC tried to break it up DJ dropped the gun and he just remember hearing 3 loud pops. He didn't know he actually shot him. Desmond and DJ was so close growing up. Talonda couldn't believe it gotten to a point that would cause them fight and try to kill one another. Talonda sat there with her second oldest and kept saying she's not mad at him and she loves him so much. On the other hand she wanted to know why DJ would do that to his own sister. She really didn't know if she was sad or angry about everything. She kept asking herself why. She knew that question would never get answered. She asked Desmond, "Do you want to attend the funeral?" Desmond told his mom, "I'm hurting so bad on the inside and I couldn't face the fact my brother will be laying in a casket because of me." "The person I really wanted to kill was Dre."

Talonda told Desmond, "I'm done with Dre and he won't be coming around anymore." Desmond looked at his mom and told her, "The only thing Dre gone be doing is pushing up weeds." Talonda looked at Desmond with a side eye. Desmond said, "Ma Dre got killed, they found him in an abandoned house by the court." Talonda looked at Desmond and said "Please tell me you didn't!" Desmond said "No ma!" "I had nothing to do with that!" Talonda raise her head to the ceiling while saying "Thank You GOD" in a very soft tone. Desmond noticed his mom really didn't care about too much about Dre getting killed. Maybe because she's more focused on their situation. Talonda knew she had to break the news to her mother and tell her the truth about everything. She was afraid that she will have a heart attack instead of a stroke. She knew her dad couldn't handle the loss his grandson. If he knew half of what's been going on he would have been passed away. Talonda just sat there and held her son. She knew if Desmond went to prison she would be losing another son. Just not to the undertaker. Desmond couldn't seem to pull himself together.

He just kept crying and asking GOD to forgive him and his sins. Desmond begged and pleaded with GOD for his forgiveness. He really wasn't trying to kill his brother. He loved his brother deeply. Desmond knew a lot of people saw what happened and he knew they would probably come to the funeral. They met a lot of people through LOC and Dead Eye, but he didn't know if they would still talk to the police. Desmond knew it wouldn't disappear, and he had nowhere to run. They family wasn't that big and he didn't know his dad's side of the family. He decided that he will turn his self in after the funeral. He told his mom what his decision was. She didn't want her son to go to jail. Desmond didn't want to go back home. He wanted to stay at the hotel until he turned his self in. Tracey agreed to pay for the room for him. Tracey looked at her nieces and nephews like they were her own children because she didn't have any. So she was feeling Talonda's pain also. They use to be a close nit family until Talonda steered into another direction. Tracey was gone be there for her nephew as much as she could. Talonda told Desmond, "I got to leave so I could break the news to Moma and Daddy." She told him, "I need to be at the house for when they call to see which funeral home I want the morgue to release DJ's body to."

Chapter 8

Three days has passed since DJ's death. The morgue released his body and ruled his death as a homicide. So now it was time for Talonda to plan his funeral arrangements. Her case manager from the center raised $5000.00 dollars for DJ's funeral and Tracey help pay for everything else. Desmond had the money for his brother's funeral but that was the last thing on his mind. Talonda decided not to tell her parents until DJ's body was released to the funeral home. She knew her mom was gone want to go and see him to see if it was really her grandson. Talonda and Tracey broke the news to their parents together. Tracey consoled their dad while Talonda consoled their mother. They took the news pretty hard. Moma Tanya held herself together; she wanted to see Desmond to make sure he was okay. Talonda sat at the house with her dad while Tracey took Moma Tanya to the hotel to see Desmond. Everyone was so wrapped around the situation. They forgot to check on Shelley and the kids.

When Tracey and Moma Tanya made it to the hotel and Desmond saw his granny. He broke down worse than he did when he saw his mother. He didn't have to worry about explaining the story because his mom and aunt did it for him. It still didn't make him feel no better. He didn't have an appetite his concious was eating away at him. All he could do was pace the room and pray. He was scared to go to sleep because he kept visualizing the incident in his head. Every time he closed his eyes he saw DJ's face. While he was in there with his grandmother Krystal kept calling him and he didn't have the energy to talk to anyone except his family. Moma Tanya prayed for Desmond and he told her that's was all he been doing was praying, and he will feel better once he turned himself in. Moma Tanya was gone make sure Desmond had the best Attorney there was. She just lost one grandson; she didn't want to lose another one. They looked at the fact Desmond was protecting his sister, not the bigger picture that he killed DJ.

Desmond was really a good kid. He followed DJ's path and DJ ended up changing on him. Desmond felt like if DJ only talked to him from jump all of this could have been avoided. Desmond knew DJ tried to kill him, so he started to feel like if LOC wasn't there to wrestle the gun out of DJ's hand he would be the one getting buried. Their family considered it to be self-defense but he knew LOC wasn't gone get involved in no police shit. Tracey knew her and Talonda had to start the arrangements for the funeral. She asked Desmond if he wanted to go to Moma Tanya's house and sit with her and grandpa until they came back. He wanted to go because he didn't want to be alone but he was afraid the police would come over there looking for him. Mentally he wanted to turn his self in, but he was scared to go to jail. He really wanted to see his brothers and sisters because he knew once he went to jail it would a long time before he saw them again. Moma Tanya told Tracey to go get the kids and take them to her house while she sits with Desmond. She didn't want to leave him alone. She knew he was terrified. Moma Tanya sat and held her grandson trying to keep him calm so he wouldn't do anything to harm himself. Moma Tanya ordered and pizza and had Tracey pick it up she didn't want to use her credit or debit card in case the police was looking for Desmond. When Tracey came back with the pizza Desmond still couldn't eat. All he would do is drink water.

The nervousness kept making his mouth dry. Moma Tanya tried to get him to eat a lil but he just couldn't. He kept thinking about DJ and all the things that could happen to him if he went to prison. He wasn't no tough dude. He knew it was dudes in there was way bigger than he was.

He saw what could happen to people in prison on TV. He didn't want to end up being another niggas bitch. With all the anger he had built up inside of him he was more scared that he would kill again even in prison if he had to. After hearing what happened to his sisters he wasn't gone let no nigga rape him and get away with it. Then again if niggas held him down then what would he do? He just kept thinking about everything that could go wrong in jail and everything that could go in his favor. He knew he didn't want to kill his brother but would the judge believe it was self-defense.

Every time he closed his eyes and opened them he thought he was waking up from a dream. Until he looked around and realized everything was reality. Moma Tanya went home to check on grandpa and feed him. In the meantime the word spread about DJ's death and everyone started to come over Talonda's house and bring food and offer their condolences. Tracey decided to handle as much as she could so Talonda could be at home when people stop by. One of Talonda's old co-workers stopped over to offer her help. Krystal's mother brought some chicken and pop over on behalf of her family. Krystal thought Desmond would be there so she could console him but he wasn't there. Talonda was getting a lot of spiritual support from everyone in the neighborhood. The detective stopped by and brought Talonda DJ's cell phone and the money he had in his pocket. He also asked Talonda if he could speak with her. Talonda got nervous she just knew he was going to ask her where Desmond was.

He wanted to talk to her about the drugs he found in DJ's pocket. Talonda told the Detective that she was a recovering addict. She was actually away in a treatment facility when her son was killed. She had no clue that he was involved in drugs. The detective told her that DJ's Death was probably drug related. Just discussing the situation made Talonda break down into tears. The Detective decided to leave he didn't want to upset her no more that she already was. He told her if she hears anything to feel free to call him. Talonda nodded her head and walked the Detective to the door. She felt a lil good knowing they still didn't know it was Desmond that did it. She knew no one had said anything as of yet. She thought maybe Desmond would come home knowing they think it was drug related and no one told on him. Desmond wasn't ready to go home because he didn't want to see the pictures of DJ in the house everything at home reminded him of his brother. He couldn't go to his granny house because she had pictures too. He was seeing DJ every time he closed his eyes, even when he blinked his eyes. He couldn't bare to see the site of anything else. LOC called and checked on him, but Dead Eye never called to see if he was good or anything.

He knew Dead Eye knew about it because LOC knew. Desmond stayed in the hotel until the day of the funeral. LOC came up to the hotel to see Desmond the day before the funeral and brought him an airbrushed T-shirt with the picture they took together on DJ's birthday. When Desmond saw the t-shirt he smirked because they had so much fun together that day. That was the DJ he knew and loved so much. He didn't know who this other DJ was. DJ did a 360, he cut Desmond off like he wasn't even his brother. LOC told Desmond, "You will stress yourself out more trying to figure why DJ started acting the way he was acting." Desmond told LOC, "You know Tootie never called my mom to pay her respects." His mom mentioned to him everybody that stopped by or called but she never mentioned her name not once. Even though she didn't know Tootie was fucking her son. The entire time DJ was alive she stayed under him, now he's gone she is nowhere to be found. LOC told Desmond, "That bitch was only out for some money she didn't give a fuck about DJ." "As long as he supplied everything that bitch was cool." "I think Tootie turned DJ on to sum get high shit, that's why he was tripping like he was."

When Desmond brought up what DJ did to his sister he instantly began to have thoughts like LOC. Maybe Tootie did have DJ out there doing some shit. Desmond said to himself. Everything was fucked up in Desmond's life. He started to feel like maybe going to jail he would be able to escape it all. LOC told him he will never escape it. He needs to find a way to move forward. He can't undo what's already done. Desmond ask LOC if he could change what he did that sent him to prison would he. LOC told him "HELL NO"! "I had to feed my family". Desmond had to understand his situation was different that wasn't pertaining to drugs and that he killed his brother. Desmond asked LOC what would be the worst-case scenario if he went to jail. LOC told him although it was self-defense it's gone be hard to prove it. LOC said he can get a few hypes to speak up on his behalf because DJ did shoot first. He don't know how it will play out but it's worth a try.

Desmond told LOC he will pay them to come to court and tell what happened. After all they not really snitching because it was the truth. LOC told Desmond he will handle it so he won't have to spend no money in case he will need it. Talking to LOC made Desmond feel so much better. After LOC left Desmond was able to get a lil sleep. He hadn't been to sleep since the day everything happened. His eyes were red and swollen from crying so much. Talonda went back up to the hotel to sit with Desmond awhile before the funeral tomorrow. She walked in the room and saw her baby laying there sleep holding the t-shirt dedicated to his brother. She brought him a matching suit to wear so he would be matching DJ. She thought that would've made him feel just a tad bit better. When they were little boys she use to dress them alike all the time and they would tell people they were twins. Desmond could hear his mom's movement in the room so he woke up and she showed him the suit she got for him to wear. "This is the same exact one DJ is getting buried in." Stated Talonda. Desmond didn't feel like he deserved to dress like his brother. He is responsible for his death why should he be giving the opportunity to dress like him. Desmond felt like him and DJ had become enemies. DJ just cut him the fuck off without a reason why.

They went from talking and hanging every day to not talking and seeing each other for days. Talonda knew she needed counseling for herself and all her children because they was definitely gone need it. They have been through so much it was gone take a lot to repair their broken home. She blames herself for everything that has went on because if she was there for her children none of this would have happened to any of them. She never wanted her daughters to go through what she had gone through. She hurts so badly because their innocence has been taking and she can't give it back to them. She felt like she should be the one turning herself in after the funeral not Desmond. Desmond was curious to know if Tootie stopped by or called. "Has Tootie been over to see you?" Asked Desmond. "I haven't heard from her in almost five years." Replied Talonda. Desmond knew Tootie couldn't face his mom. He decided not to tell his mom Tootie was fucking around with DJ. It wasn't gone bring him back or make the situation better. "Mom do you think I will get killed one day?" Talonda grabbed her son and hugged and said, "NO"! "Desmond don't think or talk like that". "Mom do you believe in karma?" "I do, but in this case it was a mistake you didn't mean to kill your brother." "All you have to do was ask GOD for his forgiveness." "My parents always told me our GOD is a forgiving GOD." Replied Talonda.

Desmond felt like GOD wasn't gone forgive him because he never called on him til now. Talonda prayed for healing for her son and her entire family. Desmond realized that everything could've went differently but it was too late to think of how it could've went. "Do you want to stay at home since the funeral is tomorrow?" Asked Talonda. He decided to go home with his mother and spend time with his family because that Monday morning he was gone turn his self in. When Desmond got home Shelly ran and gave him a big hug. She was so happy to see him. She didn't know how everything went down between DJ and Desmond but she did find out that Desmond killed him from listening to her mom and aunt talk. Desmond told Shelly "after the funeral I'm gone probably have to leave for a long time and I want you to take care of mom and the kids like you've been doing." "Make sure you go to school and go to college so you can become somebody."

DJ was already gone, he possibly was about to go to prison for the rest of his life. He wanted his sister to make better choices and decisions for herself. Shelly was so heart broken. She didn't want her brother to go to jail. She started crying and telling Desmond "you can't go you said you will always be here to protect me." Desmond tried told hold back his tears but Shelly hit a soft spot in him when she said that. Whenever she had nightmares he always told her he would always be there to protect her. That made him feel more fucked up. He felt like he should've stayed at the hotel. He was more worried about what people was gone say when he walked in the funeral. Now he is worried about what all could happen to his brothers and sisters while he's gone. Desmond and DJ was very close but Desmond and Shelly was always closer than DJ and Shelly was. "I'm kind of happy DJ is dead because I was scared of him." Said Shelly. "Don't think like that, he was still your brother and you should never wish death on no one." Replied Desmond.

He understood how she felt but he wanted her to look at the situation totally different. He felt like she was giving him props for killing their oldest brother. "I thought you told me people who hurt kids should burn in hell." "Don't that goes for DJ too?" Replied Shelly. "I know I said that but it's a lil different because that's our brother." Replied Desmond. "Why is it any different for him than anyone else?" Asked Shelly. Shelley was really confusing Desmond he knew what she meant but he didn't want her to think its okay to kill a family member. "One day you will understand where I'm coming from with all this." Said Desmond. "If I write a letter to the jail would they let you come home?" Asked Shelly. He smirked and said, "naw I don't think it will be that easy." Desmond talked to Shelly for a lil while longer. He knew Shelly was the only person he could trust leaving all his money with, besides she had an account she opened with the help of the school for students with good grades. He told Shelly he wanted her to keep his money in her account because he didn't trust nobody else to keep his money. Shelly would do anything for her brother. The funeral started at 1:00pm. Desmond asked LOC, "Can you take me and Shelly up to the bank when they open at 10:00?"

Desmond told Shelly, "no matter what happens to me I want to make sure yall are good." He was gone give the rest of his dope to LOC when he came to pick them up that morning. He didn't want his mom to come in contact with no type of drugs. Talonda had been doing well so far, but he didn't know how she was gone be once he went to jail. It started getting late and Desmond had to prepare his self mentally for the funeral tomorrow. He knew sleeping was not an option. He sat up and watched TV on the couch he didn't want to sleep in his bed because he shared rooms with DJ. Looking at DJ's things was just too painful for him. While he was watching TV Krystal sent him a text. She didn't want to bother calling him because she knew it was a difficult time for him and his family. At first he wasn't gone read the text but he did.

The text read:

> *I am sending my prayers to you and your family. I know tomorrow is going to be a difficult time for you all. I pray GOD gives you all the strength and heal all open wounds. I am here if you ever need to talk or an ear to listen. I can't promise you that everything is going to be okay. But I know GOD is with you every step of the way.*

Desmond text her back and said.

I appreciate that and it means a lot.

He knew once she found out the truth she would regret sending him that message. He always liked her and now he finally had the chance to get to know her he messed it all up. He broke down into tears wishing he could turn the hands on the clock backwards. He would do anything to have his brother back. Desmond genuinely loved his brother. He regretted they ever started selling dope and making money. He felt like drugs and money came between him and his brother. All wanted to do was be able to provide for their family. DJ let the power of a money get the best of him and it changed who he really was. He went from having nothing to having everything a person could want at their age. He let Tootie have too much control over him. She knew she could manipulate him because she had hella street sense. Tootie use to con niggas out of everything and get niggas for their money.

Everybody wanted to fuck her because she was cute and thick as hell. She had total pussy control when it came to almost any nigga. If she wanted something she was determined to get it. Some of them caught on to her ass and went upside her head but it didn't stop her. DJ was right up her alley because he was young and she knew him personally so she know how to come to him because he trusted her. DJ didn't treat her like he did them other bitches. Tootie knew all his business and DJ knew she wasn't shit even as a child he use to see her with different dudes. It really fucked Desmond head up when DJ told him he was knocking her off. Desmond knew if his mom ever found out she was fucking DJ she would end up locked up right with him. His mom stop hanging around her sum years ago, because she started lacing her weed. That's like calling the kettle black because she started using dope too. He knew his mom wouldn't look at it that way. She would be pissed because she was their godmother and she was fucking her godson.

Desmond was thinking of everything he could to get it all out before he turned himself in. He wanted to go to jail with a clear head. One minute he can seem to pull it together the next minute he would burst into tears. He knew he was gone have to live with killing his brother for the rest of his life. Talonda got up to get a drink of water she saw DJ sitting on the couch, she went over to see if he was okay. She knew he really wasn't. It was killing her to see her son go through all this. She had the wake and funeral in the same day because that would be too much for Desmond to handle. During all this she has not thought about getting high at all. She was too worried about what was gone happen to her son and she knew she had to be there for him. She called her counselors daily so they could help keep her on the right track. After seeing her mother have a stroke and losing her son she didn't want to fuck up and lose her family. She and Tracey has gotten back close since all this has happened.

Talonda couldn't sleep either. She sat and held Desmond and watched TV with him until the both of them dozed off together. Desmond felt safe in his mother's arms. Desmond woke up about six that morning and took a shower. He knew everybody had to get in before the funeral. While he was in the shower Talonda was up making breakfast for everybody. This was the day Desmond dreaded. He didn't want to face the public and he definitely didn't want to see his brother like that. Desmond was sadder the day of the funeral more than he was the day everything happened. He knew that was the last day he would ever see his brothers face again. Besides when he comes into his dreams. When LOC showed up the morning of the came in and gave Talonda a hug and told her, "I'm sorry for her loss." Talonda smiled and told him "thank you." LOC took Desmond and Shelly to the bank while Talonda was in the shower so he could deposit his money into her account. LOC could see it in Desmond's face he was taking it real hard. LOC asked Desmond, "Do you want me to walk in the funeral with you, so you won't feel like its tension in the air?"

That made Desmond feel a lil better but not too much. Shelly told him, "I would be there to hold your hand every step of the way." After leaving the bank they went back to crib and awaited his granny, grandpa and aunt to arrive before the funeral cars came to pick up the family. LOC hadn't seen Tracey since Christmas. They exchanged numbers but it didn't go too far between them. Desmond didn't want to ride with the family he wanted to ride with LOC instead. Desmond asked LOC, "Have you hollered at Dead Eye?" "He said yeah he will be there." Replied LOC.

His grandparents and Aunt arrived at the house 30 minutes before the funeral director came. Desmond hadn't seen his grandpa in a while so he was happy to see him. His grandpa didn't know he killed DJ he just knew DJ had been killed. Moma Tanya gave her grandson big hug and a kiss and told him, "I've been praying for you and I love you so much." Everybody knew this was gone be a hard day for Desmond.

The Funeral Director pulled up at the house to get the family. Shelly asked, "Can I ride with yall Desmond?" LOC was cool with her riding with them to the funeral and LOC walked in with the family. He was family to Desmond. He was the only person that hadn't turned on him so far. When everyone made it to the church and it was time for the family to walk in.

Desmond felt sick to his stomach. He started vomiting outside by the door. LOC told Talonda, "Me and Shelly got him." He okay you can go ahead and walk in with Tracey." Instead of them walking in a pair of two's when Desmond was about to walk in Shelly was on one side holding his hand and LOC walk on the other side of him. When they reach the casket for their final viewing Shelly kissed her brother on his forehead despite what he had done to her. She didn't want to see him like that. She did love her brother. Desmond laid his head on Desmond's chest and told his brother how much he loved him and was gone miss him. He wished it had of been him instead of DJ. Desmond didn't want to leave the casket. LOC had to pull him away. Desmond was crying so hard he didn't even pay attention that LOC had been there earlier that morning to view DJ and put the same t-shirt he had given him in DJ's casket.

Tracey made sure her nephew was put away damn good. He casket was baby blue with silver plated tips. DJ was dressed in all cream with a silver and baby blue tie. Desmond was dressed identical to his brother. DJ looked like he was sleeping not dead. During the funeral while the preacher was preaching Desmond had his head down and he felt a cool breeze blow past him all of a sudden, he raised his head because he thought someone was fanning him but they wasn't. He saw DJ raise his head from the casket and say to him in very soft tone. *"It's okay Des!"* *"Don't cry!"* *"I'm at peace!"* *"I will always love you lil bro!"* Desmond jumped up and blurted out "NO!" "NO!" "DJ!" "DON'T GO!" When he calmed down and looked over at the casket again DJ was still laying there like he was asleep. Talonda went and sat next to Desmond he was crying out so loud he was louder than the preacher. Talonda did everything she could to calm him down but nothing was working he cried through the entire service.

Shelly held his hand all the way through but he was hurting too bad. Desmond's heart was totally broken. The other kids really didn't know what was going but they knew something was wrong. They were looking at everyone else cry so they started crying. Moma Tanya and Tracey calmed them down as much as they could.

Talonda didn't know so many people knew her kids. The church was wall to wall packed with people. Her old boss that fired her even showed up to pay his respects to Talonda and her family. Desmond saw Dead Eye standing by the wall. He got up and walked over to him and gave him a hug. They hugged one another so tight they didn't wanna let each other go. Dead Eye whispered in Desmond's ear, "I love you dude, and I'm sorry for everything that has happened." Desmond shook his head and told Dead Eye, "I love you back fam." He went back and sat next to his mother and sister. The services at the church were coming to an end. The preacher asked if anybody would volunteer to carry any flowers and for the pallbearers to come forward. Talonda's old co-workers came forward to carry out the flowers for the family. Talonda did have anyone listed to be a pallbearer because she didn't know any of their friends. Desmond got up, LOC got up, Dead eye walked over there and three mo dudes from the hood came to help carry they body out to the hearse. Talonda was seeing so many young dudes with DJ's picture on their shirt and she knew at that moment her son was really loved. It was about 100 cars following the hearse to the grave site. Moma Tanya paid for DJ to be buried by the plot she had already paid for her and grandpa. She actually paid for her daughters and all her grandkids to get buried by them.

When they arrived at the graves site Desmond had switched into the t-shirt LOC got made for him with their last pic together on there. After the preacher did the eulogy and the casket was getting lowered. Desmond stood there for a while longer by himself, because everyone else started walking back to their cars. Shelly was about to go over there with Desmond but LOC stopped her and said, "give him a minute, let him say his final goodbyes alone." While Desmond was standing there he felt the same breeze he felt in the church. This time DJ was sitting on top on the casket telling him, *"You can leave now!" "I'm tired!" "I'm ready to get some rest Des!"* Then he disappeared again. Desmond knew if he told anybody that DJ talked to him in the church and at the gravesite. They would think he was tripping. He waited til he got to the repast and he pulled his mom aside and said, "Ma DJ talked to me." She smiled and told Desmond, "He's your angel now and he's letting you know he forgave you and he wants you to be at peace with everything."

A couple people came up to Desmond and told him they know he didn't mean to kill his brother. They knew DJ shot at him first and they was willing to talk to whomever so he won't go to jail for the rest of his life for nothing. Just hearing the people say they knew it wasn't his fault made him feel so much better.

He thought everyone looked at him as if he was a real killer. Then to hear people say they would testify on his behalf made him feel even better. But what made him feel a sense of relief about it all was what his mom had just told him. He was actually able to eat just a little, but not too much. He hadn't really ate anything since the day it happened. Desmond decided to spend these last couple of days with his family before turning himself in.

Chapter 9

Monday morning arrived and Desmond began to have second thoughts. He wasn't sure if he wanted to turn his self in or not. If he kept running it would have only made him look guilty. He never told anyone but he had thoughts of taking his own life. Either way it wouldn't bring DJ back. The time started changing faster and faster. LOC made it to his house around 8:30 in the morning to get Desmond and Talonda, so they could take him in. Desmond hugged all his sisters and brothers and told them how much he loved them and don't ever forget him. Shelly took it the hardest because they were so close. Desmond was trying to be strong but Shelly made him break down. LOC told Desmond, "Get all yo crying out the way while you at the crib." "You can't go in there crying, and try not to focus on what's going out here in these streets, cuz it ain't shit you can do about it."

Desmond hadn't never been away from him family before. Shelly wanted to go with him so bad, but she had to stay and watch the kids. LOC told Desmond while they was still at the crib "Try to eat you a lil something because they don't feed you worth shit behind them walls." "The only way you eat descent is if you got money on yo books." Don't worry about no bread you gone be good lil nigga." Desmond's stomach was full of butterflies, he was too nervous to eat. Talonda told Desmond, "No matter what happened I'm gone continue to stay clean and be there for you every step of the way." Dead Eye called Desmond's phone and told him to keep his head up and he will make sure he's good while he's in there. It was time for them to go. They wanted to go before shifts changed because the booking officers worked split shifts. They didn't want him to be sitting in booking for hours waiting to get booked. Once they arrived at Bulletin County. Desmond held his held up and walked in the county ready to just get it all over with. He knew in his heart he was doing the right thing. They sat and waited for a clerk or somebody to come to the window.

After an hour passed no one had shown up yet. The longer he sat waiting the more he was getting frustrated and started having second thoughts. They sat there for about 30 more minutes then finally an officer came to the window and asked, "Have you all been helped?" Desmond looked over at his mom with a slight frown as he got up and walked over to the window and told the officer, I'm there to turn himself in for killing his brother." The officer asked Desmond, who is your brother?" He said. "DJ." Then cleared his throat and said excuse me, "D'Wayne Thompson." The officer asked Desmond, "Is you talking about the young man that was killed about a week ago?" Desmond responded, "Yes ma'am." The officer was kind of puzzled because the report stated it was drug related and there was no information on a suspect. She told Desmond, "Have a seat while I contact the detective over the case." They sat there for about an hour, but it felt like forever to Desmond. Then the officer came back to the window and told Desmond and his family the detective handling the case was out in the field, but another detective will be out to talk to them. They waited for about another 15 minutes. Then a tall white man with a deep voice said can I help you all.

Desmond, his mom and LOC walked over to the window together and Desmond told the detective he wanted to turn his self in for killing his brother. The detective told Desmond, "I'm gone unlock the door for you and your parents." He needed to get a statement from Desmond but a parent had to be there because he was a minor. Everyone introduced themselves and the detective introduced his self as Det. Longhorn. He advised Desmond and his mom of his rights and told him, "You are not under arrest at this moment but your statement was going to be recorded." He asked Talonda and LOC, "Do you all give him permission to voluntary give his statement?" Talonda replied, "yes I do." The detective told Desmond, "Start from the beginning and tell him what lead up to you killing your brother." Desmond didn't tell him about all the prior stuff. He started off telling the detective what Shelly said happened. He said, "Hearing what my sister said our brother did to her really upset me sir." The same sister and my other two sister was molested by our mom's ex-boyfriend who is also deceased." Talonda had a look of shame all over her face.

Desmond told the Detective, When I saw DJ sitting in the car I walked over to him and hit him in his jaw." "DJ jumped out the car and ran up on me and we started fighting." "DJ ran to the car he was in and retrieved a gun." "He shot at me like 3 maybe 4 times." "I hid behind a park car." "Someone wrestle the gun out of DJ's hand then the gun hit the ground." "I ran and pick the gun up off the ground and the next thing I heard was 2 maybe 3 pops." "I couldn't remember shooting because everything happened so fast." Desmond started to cry as he explained the incident more to Det. Longhorn on his account of how things happened. He told the detective, "I didn't know I actually shot my brother." "All of a sudden everything was quiet and everyone started to move in slow motion as if the where mimes or something." "Then I saw my brother on the ground bleeding." "I walked over to him and tried to help him." "That's when I was able to hear all the screaming and yelling from everyone." "I couldn't remember if his eyes were open or closed." "I got nervous and jumped on my bike and took off." "I didn't know where I was going." "I was just riding until my feet couldn't paddle anymore." Desmond started to break down more and more.

His tears were coming down uncontrollably. Talonda put her arm around him, so she could console him. Desmond told the detective in a very remorseful voice. "I am very sorry and I never meant to kill my brother." "I'm not a murderer Detective." "Me and him was together every day." "I know what I did was wrong, and I'm here to deal with the consequences of my actions." Desmond dropped his head as if he couldn't speak anymore. He didn't know what else to say it was gone bring DJ back nor make the situation any better. The detective asked Desmond, what did you do with the gun?" Desmond replied, "I don't know!" "I just remember dropping the gun and running over to my brother." The detective asked Desmond, how old are you?" Desmond responded, "16 almost 17." "My brother was 18 almost 19." The detective ask Desmond to wait out in the hall on the bench while he talks to his parents. Desmond was a lil confused. The detective told him he wasn't under arrest in the beginning and now he's talking to his mom and LOC without him. He didn't want his mom to tell the detective LOC wasn't his father because LOC knew how the system works and he wanted him to hear everything.

It was too late she told the detective that LOC was like an uncle to Desmond and DJ. They didn't know their real dad. She was molested when she got pregnant with the both of them. She told the detective she has 5 other kids and Desmond and DJ was a big help to her. The detective explained to Talonda that he was going to have to put Desmond under arrest because it is a murder and it was ruled a homicide. He also told her that he would be booking him as a juvenile but it's up to the district attorney and the prosecutor to determine if they want to charge him as an adult. He also advised her that by them not having any suspects and Desmond came in on his own free will to turn his self in which would look good in his favor. The entire time they were in there Desmond heart and mind was racing. He couldn't hear and he didn't know what was going on.

The detective advised Talonda that if the family couldn't afford an attorney one would be issued to him through the courts. LOC spoke up and said, "We will hire him a personal attorney if he needs one." Talonda looked over at LOC because she knew she didn't have the money for a personal attorney. Attorney's that represent murder cases are very expensive. Although her mom said she would hire him the best attorney there is. It could cost well-over $10,000.00 depending how long the cases goes to court. LOC ask the detective, "Could we speak to Desmond before you take him into custody?" The detective agreed that it was ok for them to have a minute with him. When Talonda and LOC walked out in the hallway Desmond looked kind of blank. He thought his mom was going come out smiling, and ready to take him home. That was definitely not the case because he saw the tears in her eyes. He knew at that very moment he was staying.

Desmond was so terrified to go to the county. He knew it was dudes twice his size in there. Then he thought about it maybe they won't bother him because he's in there for murder. Then again they might bother him, because he did sum coward shit and killed his own brother. He was so confused, but he knew he had to pull himself together and he had to do it quick. When LOC told him that he will be going to juvenile for the time being you can see his entire facial expression change. He knew he might see some of the lil niggas from the hood up in there. Desmond thought he would do all his time in juvenile. Til his mom crushed him and said if the prosecutors decided to wave it to adult court then you would have to go to the county until sentencing. He dropped his head with frustration again. LOC told him, "Don't trip if you go to the county youngsta you know I got peeps everywhere." "You gone be good there too." "Besides I got connects on the inside so you won't have to worry about shit." To Desmond it was easy said than done. Cuz neither one of them had to do them time. The detective came out and told them that the juvenile officer was there to get Desmond. He gave his mom a hug, a kiss and told her he loved her.

He gave LOC and hug and told him he loved him also. He asked LOC, "Can you make sure my family straight?" LOC told him, "I will definitely do that for you." The guard took Desmond into custody. Talonda just stood there and watched her baby walk through the doors with the guard. It took everything out of her not to cry in front of him. When Talonda made it to the car she broke down about everything. She was only trying to hold it together to stay strong for Desmond. LOC tried talking to Talonda to encourage to be strong not only for her kids but for herself. Desmond really needed her now and he was depending on her. LOC was fucked up about Desmond going to jail because he looked at him like he was his own son or nephew. He knew Desmond was a good kid despite him trying to get a hustle for himself. He was starting to regret ever bring DJ and Desmond into the dope game with him and Dead Eye. LOC starting venting to Talonda about how he went to prison and lost his family. Talonda didn't even know LOC had ever been to jail less long had kids. LOC opened up to Talonda because he was trying to get her to see that she was not the only person going through shit. "I think about my kids often and I don't have a clue where they are." "That's why I took to DJ and Desmond." "I apologized for having them selling dope." "I only did it to help them out." Talonda appreciated him helping out her kids but she never wanted them to live that type of lifestyle. Talonda brought up the subject about her fucking Dead Eye.

LOC just listened he never mentioned her that Desmond told him about him. "I regret fucking with Dead Eye." "It hurted Desmond so bad when he caught us together." "Regardless of my drug usage I never meant to hurt my kids." "That rat bastard Dre was molesting my daughters and I was blindsided by it." "I felt like Dre was keeping me high so he could fuck with my daughters." Replied Talonda. LOC told Talonda, "well that's one problem you will never have to worry about again." Talonda told LOC, "I wish I could meet the person who took his life because the way I feel now, I would have took his life myself." LOC just nodded his head agreeing with Talonda. Although they were having a deep conversation LOC never would say too much. He didn't believe in telling bitches none of his business. He always felt like they talk too fucking much and they will either get you killed or sent to prison with their fucking mouth. The crazy part is LOC never told Desmond he was the one who killed Dre. When Desmond told him how Dre was molesting his lil sisters.

LOC tried to keep him leveled headed so he wouldn't end up in the position he is in now. When Desmond was at home Dre came by the spot to get 2 bags. LOC trunked that nigga and took him to the abandoned house and made that nigga get on his knees and popped him in the back of his head. He knew they wouldn't try to find out who killed him because he was a dope head. Anything that's drug related becomes a cold case unless it involves little children or the elderly. That's a secret he will take to his grave. He didn't tell even mention it to Dead Eye. He saw the hurt and pain in Desmond's eyes when he was telling him about it. LOC was locked up with child molesters and rapist, he despise them motherfuckers. He hated any nigga or bitch that fucked with helpless kid and old folk. When he was in the joint they kept molesters and rapist together they wasn't allowed into population. Talonda hadn't never been to jail herself so she didn't know what it was like. If she could have, she woulda did Desmond's time for him in a heartbeat.

She didn't want Desmond to turn himself in. It wasn't like she didn't know who killed DJ. As long as the police didn't have any suspects in mind she wanted Desmond to let it go. But his conscious was killing him rapidly. Talonda missed so much out her kids' lives during the time she was getting high. The moment she goes and try to get herself together another tragedy strikes. She just sat in car on her way home thinking of all the things that could have avoided all this. LOC didn't say too much to her, he knew her mind was cluttered. When he dropped her off he gave her his number and told her, "You can call if you ever needed to talk or needed anything." Even though LOC was a street nigga he gained a lot of knowledge being in the joint. When Talonda was getting out of the car. LOC was checking her out, he could see why Dead Eye wanted to knock her off. She was a sexy motherfucker. She just fucked with the wrong type of niggas. LOC knew Desmond respected him a lot and he tried talking to his aunt Tracey so he had to get those thoughts about Talonda out his head. When he got back to the spot he saw Tootie sitting there chilling with Dead Eye. LOC and Dead Eye knew she called herself fucking around with DJ while he was alive.

She was just like all them other bitches in the street. She wanted to hang around any niggas she thought had money and would get her high for free. She didn't even have the audacity to show up at DJ's funeral but the whole time he was alive she stayed up under that nigga. LOC didn't trust the bitch, he knew her from awhile back. He couldn't understand why Dead Eye would bring her ass into their spot like that. He wanted to check Dead Eye about the shit, but he wanted to holla at him when he was by his self. Tootie chilled for about 15 minutes, then she noticed the tension coming from LOC so she got paranoid and left. She told Dead

Eye, "Catch up with me later." "I got sum moves to make." He nodded his head at her as if he really didn't give a fuck is she left or not. Once she left LOC checked Dead Eye about bringing her to the crib. Dead Eye had that cocky ass attitude like he could do whatever because he was the one who put LOC, DJ and Desmond on.

He told LOC, "Unc this my shit and I could bring whoever I wanted too up in this bitch!" LOC said, "yeah I know this yo shit nephew but you know what we got going on so why would you bring a bitch like that up in here!" Dead Eye said, "the bitch was trying to suck my dick!" "I just wanted sum head from the hoe!" LOC said, "damn man DJ ain't been dead a week now you gone fuck his old bitch!" "You was just fucking his moma!" Dead Eye said, "Unc these hoes for everybody!" "I don't love these bitches!" LOC knew Dead Eye ain't give a fuck but he at least he thought he respected DJ even though he was a youngsta. LOC always live by the street code "RESPECT!" Especially when it came to a nigga you fucked with on a regular. Dead Eye didn't give no fuck if he wanted to fuck a bitch he was fucking her. He left and came back with this lil bitch named Tammy he use to fuck around with back in the day. He met her while he was in foster care. She accused him of getting her pregnant but they never took a test. Tammy wasn't from his neighborhood. She got her section 8 and moved into an apartment a couple blocks down.

Dead Eye knew she was a gullible bitch and she would fuck with any nigga that was trying to hit. He didn't trust going to her crib so he told her to come to the spot and chill with him there. He didn't give two shits about her but he remembered she had some good pussy and she would suck a nigga's dick until his toes curled. He wanted to see if she still had those same skills. Tammy wasn't all that cute she just had a fat ass and sum big titties. She could fuck for hours and her pussy stayed wet the whole time. LOC hadn't seen her before but she looked like a potentially good girl. She had looked like she had something going for herself, so he thought. But he knew that if she was fucking with Dead Eye she was fucked up somewhere down the line. Dead Eye didn't waste no time he wasn't trying to chill or cuddle.

He just wanted to hit and quit. Dead Eye took Tammy straight to the room and instantly pulled his pants down and told her to get on her knees for old time sake. Tammy didn't hesitate because she enjoyed pleasing any nigga she had the chance to please. She thought her skills as so on point that one day she would dominate a nigga with her head game. Sucking dick wasn't knew to Dead Eye he had all types of hoes begging to give him sum head because he had some money. Tammy started sucking Dead Eye's dick and she moaned as if he was pleasing her instead. She looked at him with a slight grin on her face because she knew he was enjoying it. She monitored how good it felt to him by watching his facial expressions. She sucked his dick so good that he nutted instantly and she continued to suck it, he was starting to feel weak and pushing her head back trying to get her to stop because it was feeling so good to him.

The feel was too overwhelming she continued to suck him some more and made him nut again. He has never had a bitch to suck his dick and make him nut twice. Once she was done she wanted Dead Eye to fuck her but he got his nut off and his dick wouldn't get hard. Tammy didn't like that at all. She wanted to feel his hardness inside of her. Tammy laid across the pool table that was in the room they was in and started playing with her pussy. Hoping it would make him get stiff. She grabbed his hand and started sucking on his fingers. She sucked his middle finger the most because it was his longest finger. She got it nice and moist and took his finger and rubbed across her warm wet clit. Dead Eye ain't never had a bitch to do all that freaky shit Tammy was doing. She was starting to make him get a lil hard, but he wanted to see what other tricks she could pull out her bag.

Tammy stood on top of the pool table and danced a lil for him. She squatted down on the pool table in a sitting position and like stuck he finger deep inside her womb and started riding her own finger like it was a dick. Dead Eye was getting introduced into some freaky shit for real. She then laid on her back and started licking her nipples and playing with her pussy until she made her pussy squirt lil bit. Dead Eye ain't never seen a bitch make her own pussy squirt before. He was getting turned on by that shit. Tammy told Dead Eye, "tell yo boy to come and join the party it's enough to go around." Dead Eye knew his uncle wasn't game for no shit like that. He told her, "I want all this to myself." She said, "I can tell you ain't acting like it." She noticed them rock hard arms LOC had and his sexy build. She just knew he had a pipe in his pants and she wanted to feel some of it. She told Dead Eye, "I like sucking dick and getting fucked at the same time." Dead Eye responded "DAMNNN"! "So you like threesomes huh?" She told him, "hell yeah I only live once." He asked her, "Would you have a threesome with another woman involved?"

She looked at Dead Eye and told him, "I sure would if I can lick the pussy and the dick at the same time while you fucking her." He was definitely starting to get turned back on. He told her, "won't you dance for me a lil mo while I make this phone call and make this shit happen." He instantly called Tootie and asked her where she was at. She was down the block. He asked her if she wanted to make a couple dollars doing a threesome. Tootie asked him with who. He told her with one of his old bitches he use to fuck. Tootie said she's never did a threesome with another woman she was used to it being two dudes. But since he was paying she was playing. He fired up the piece of blunt he had left while they waited for Tootie to come back. When she knocked on the door LOC answered the door.

She asked for Dead Eye. LOC said in a smart tone, "didn't yo ass just leave here." He was about to tell her that Dead Eye was gone because he had the other bitch there. But Tootie cut him off and said, "He just called me to come back." LOC looked sexy as hell to Tootie too, but he scared her for some reason. She didn't like his attitude or the tone of his voice. That was one nigga she couldn't pursue. Tootie walked down to the room Dead Eye was in. She saw Tammy dancing on the pool table, so she started taking off her shit so she could show her skills too. She wasn't about to let no young bitch show stop her. She been in the game way too long to let a young bitch test her skills. Tootie got on the pool table and started popping her pussy while Tammy was making that ass clap for Dead Eye.

Tammy was on some freak shit though. She told Tootie, "Let's give him a real show." "Lay yo ass on the pool table so I can get between yo legs and rub my pussy up against yours." Tootie was kind of liking that shit. Tammy started sucking on her hard nipples. Tootie grabbed Tammy by the hair and pulled her up to her face and started kissing her. The sight of it all was so over whelming Dead Eye he lit up another blunt and watched them do their thang. Tammy started to move down toward Tootie's stomach and began to lick and kiss her navel. She made her way to her thighs and she couldn't resist the bald and fatness of her pussy. She swiveled her tongue across her pussy lips, giving her a lil tease. She blew on her pussy to get her aroused a lil more. Then she spread her legs wide open and over her shoulders and began to tongue kiss her pussy as if she was making love to it. Tootie let out a sexy soft moan that made Tammy suck her clit harder. Dead Eye stood behind Tammy while she licked Tootie's pussy and watched as a few drips of cum fell from her pussy lips.

Tammy sucked and sucked until Tootie was about to climax then she stopped. She didn't want her to cum just yet. Tootie was begging her to keep going. Dead Eye told Tootie now show me how you can make her pussy feel. Tootie played with Tammy's clit for a few seconds. She started to blow on it to cool her down and excite her at the same time. She started to finger her so her juices can moist her hand. The stuck two fingers in her and licked her clit while she played with her pussy. Dead Eye told Tootie, "lick on dat pussy a lil bit for me too." Tootie began to lick and suck Tammy's pussy. She was making wet sucking noises with her mouth while she was sucking her pussy. When Dead Eye seen how thick, long and wide Tooties tongue was. He pulled out his dick and told her, "Come play with this dick for a while." While Tootie was sucking Dead Eyes dick he started eating Tammy's pussy. He couldn't resist how wet it was. He wanted to see if it taste as good as it looks.

He was liking how dat pussy tasted too. Tammy was licking and gagging and nibbling on the head of his dick. It was feeling so damn good to him, he was ready to stick his dick in her. He told Tootie to lay across the pool table he wanted to be able to stand up in her. Tammy couldn't get enough of Tooties head. She had a long perfect tongue that tickled the shit out of her clitoris. Tammy sat on Tootie's face while Dead Eye was fucking her. Dead Eye stuck his finger in Tammy's ass and played with her ass hole while Tootie stimulated her pussy. Dead Eye was liking the tightness of Tammy's ass and he wanted to stick his dick in there. He pulled his dick out of Tootie and told her to lick her juices on off his dick and get him back nice and hard. He told Tammy to bend over, Tammy thought he was gone fuck her in the doggy position but he went slowly inch by inch in her ass.

Tammy tensed up a lil but then she started to like the feeling of it. He stroked slow so he can feel the tightness as she gripped his dick with her ass. Her moans was started to get louder, Tootie was licking her nipples to give her more pleasure. She started to have an orgasm that she has never had before. Her body started to stiffen up as she shook and jerked letting out every ounce of cum she could produce. Dead Eye hadn't nutted yet but he was liking the feeling of fucking in the ass. As Tammy walked over to get a rag to clean herself off Dead Eye told Tootie to turn around his dick was still nice, hard and wet from Tammy's juices so he eased his dick inside Tootie's ass hole. Her ass was bigger that Tammy's so he had extra fun with her. While he was fucking Tootie in her ass, she was throwing it back at him. Dead Eye knew that wasn't her first time getting fucked in the ass. He was smaking her on her ass as she threw back at him.

She was moaning out loud telling him how good he felt inside her. Her body was starting to quiver. She started making her ass clap as she threw it back. She was fucking him like he was a real G. Tammy knew what she had to do to get her money. She was giving it to him any way he wanted it. He was fucking her so well, she started telling him that was his ass and pussy. Tammy didn't like that shit at all. She wanted that nigga for herself. Although she met a dude that was in jail and that she has been writing. But she wanted Dead Eye for the time being. Tootie was taking every inch of that dick he had to offer with no hesitation. Tootie told Dead Eye to lay on the floor, she was about to do some drastic shit. She rode him while his dick was still in her ass. She could tell Tammy was getting a lil pissed off by her performance. She rode him so good he couldn't pull out. He nutted inside her filling her ass with his cum. He told Tootie to bend over and he then told Tammy let me see you lick my nutt off of her ass.

Tammy didn't want to do it but she did it anyways so he would feel like she listens to him. Once Tammy was done she got her things and left. Tootie waited for Dead Eye to pay her, she thought she was about to get atleast $100 dollars for all that. He gave her $20.00 and told her he'll call her when he ready for another good time. Tootie couldn't do shit but take the $20.00 he gave her. Before she left she turned toward him and said "is this all you gone really give me?" He nodded his head yeah and said, "You should be happy." "I never pay bitches for pussy." "You see I ain't pay her." Tootie rolled her eyes and shook her head with frustration and left. She ain't never got played for no pussy before. When she left she was so pissed because she fucked with a bitch and let that nigga fuck her anyway he wanted and all he gave her was $20.00.

She thought since DJ hung around him that he was a sucka like DJ. If Desmond knew how Dead Eye did her he would say that's good for her ass. He couldn't stand her no more. She was with his brother every-day all day but didn't show up at his funeral. Dead Eye jumped in the shower after them bitches left and went over to one of his other bitches crib for the night. It was up to LOC and Dead Eye to be on their own shit now. Desmond and DJ was not there to do a lot of it for them. LOC was still tripping on how Dead Eye fucked Talonda and Tootie. He acted like he really didn't give a shit about the lil youngsta's. DJ and Desmond grew on LOC. He didn't trust them in the beginning but the more they came around the more he opened up to them. Most of all they listened to everything they told them and earned their trust. You would think that made a difference to Dead Eye.

All the bullshit Dead Eye been through and the type of life he had growing up. Once his moms died he didn't give a shit about anything or anybody. LOC use to feel that way back when he first went to prison. His life was on the line, He felt like the courts didn't give a fuck that he was tryna feed his family. Dead Eye lost his eye to that bullshit his mom was going through, and he wasn't there to help him or his sister. But the judge never looked at it that way. LOC was sentenced to twenty years in the pen. He was paroled that's why he was released early. Being on papers made him watch any and everything he did so he wouldn't go back, but he was doing what he had to do to survive. He never told Desmond what he went through with his case because he didn't want to scare him. LOC knew that the dope charge was damn near worse than having a murder charge.

The fact Desmond turned himself in might look good in his favor down the line or may not. It all depends on the prosecutors and the judge. For once in in LOC's life he sat down and prayed. He prayed that everything would go in Desmond's favor. He didn't want him to go through what he had gone through in his life. He saw people get murdered in jail, he saw stabbings and niggas get raped. He had a lil pull if Desmond went to the county but he knew it was some niggas in there he didn't know. He decided to reach out to this one guard he use to fuck with when he was in there waiting to get transferred to the joint. He wanted her to be on the lookout for Desmond if he came over there. She would do anything for him. She wanted to be with him but she couldn't have a relationship with passed prisoners. They remained good friends even though he wanted to get up with her a few times. He imagined making passionate love to her plenty of times. When he was in the county he just fucked her real quick to prevent from getting caught. LOC hadn't really fucked with no broads that he actually cared about since he had been out. He was well over due for a woman.

Chapter 10

LOC didn't want just any woman. He wanted a woman he could grow with. He wasn't no spring chicken no more and he wanted to build a life with someone. He was even thinking about calling Tracey and asking her out. Tracey was everything a man could ever want. He knew she wasn't going for his lifestyle. He was ready for a change. He even thought about finding him a job and leaving the streets alone. He didn't have no education besides what he got from prison. He had never had a job before. Before he went to the pen he was selling dope and he got out selling dope. His plan was to get his money up and find Porcha and his kids, but he had no way of contacting her. He contacted her mom but her mom wouldn't give him any information on them. He ran into her girl and she told him she heard she had gotten married and was living in Texas. When Porcha left she didn't want nothing else to do with LOC or Dead Eye.

She tried to raise Dead Eye as one of her own, but he insisted on doing what he wanted to do so she had nothing to do with him once he turned to the streets. Dead Eye never respected Porscha or appreciated anything she had done to help him. If it wasn't for her he would have still been in foster care. She listened to LOC and got him and he didn't appreciate it. Dead Eye was a hot head nigga, he didn't have a mother so he felt like he didn't have to listen to anyone. He use to praise his uncle because the streets knew about LOC and how he got down back in the day. Now that LOC sees life different Dead Eye feels like he's turning into a punk or something. If Dead Eye didn't want to change LOC wasn't gone try and make him. He was just gone focus on getting himself correct. LOC went to the corner store and bought a paper so he could check the job listings. Everywhere he called they wanted a resume or you had to have experience. He had neither. He knew how do a lil laborer work from a trade he picked up in prison, but that was about it.

He didn't let that discourage him, because he still had money. He wasn't into spending like Dead Eye and DJ was. That's why he was closer to Desmond they had a lot in common and he never realized it until the days leading up to Desmond to turning his self in. Dead Eye be gone pretty much every day all day. Desmond wasn't around to chill with him. LOC was starting to get bored with everything. He was sitting there thinking about Tracey quite often. He decided to hit up Talonda and holla at her. He knew she knew her sister real well and she would tell him the truth if he was wasting his time or not. He called and asked her if she thought it would be a good idea for him to ask Tracey out. Talonda thought it would be an excellent idea, considering Tracey haven't had a man in years. She told LOC, "No please ask her ass out." "I think she would like it." "She thought you were handsome when yall spent Christmas with us." "Whatever happen when yall exchanged numbers?" Asked Talonda. "I didn't think she was really interested." "I called her a few times but she was always busy so I just stopped calling." Replied LOC. Talonda explained to him that Tracey works a lot and she helps out with their dad. LOC respected that and decided to give it another try.

He asked Talonda, "What are some things she like to do or always wanted to do?" Talonda told him "just make it romantic and surprise her." Talonda told LOC, "She's actually free today she wanted to come by and watch some movies with me and the kids but I think you should call her and you spend this day with her." LOC appreciated the advice from Talonda and decided to give Tracey a call. When he called Tracey she answered the phone with an attitude, he thought that was her way of saying he was a bugga boo, but she got a new phone and didn't have his number stored into that one. LOC asked Tracey how she was doing. She responded "fine." He asked, "Are you busy?" She responded "no, but who am I talking too?" He said with a deep but sexy tone voice, "this LOC." Tracey voice and demeanor changed quickly. She said with her somewhat sexy voice "so what made you call me?" He responded, "I had been thinking about you lately and I wanted to take you out, but you be so busy." Tracey grinned and chuckled a lil bit. She said, "Well I'm not busy today." In her mind she was like yes, she been waiting so long for him to get at her.

She thought he wasn't interested in her anymore. LOC asked, "Would you like to go on a date with me?" Tracey asked, "What's the occasion was so I would know how to dress for it?" LOC told her "you already sexy, so just make sure you look sexy for me and we will go from there." LOC said, I will be ready in a few hours, I'm gone go get lined up and get my car washed, then get dressed and come to get you." Tracey was too geeked. She called Talonda real quick to her about it. Talonda told her, "I'm happy for you." She never told her that LOC called her first. Tracey was gone get dressed so she could go over to Talonda's house so she could do her makeup. When it came to beating up a face Talonda knew how to work magic with those colors. Tracey hadn't been on a date in years. She couldn't find no one that she actually liked. It was something about LOC's body that turned her own. She loved looking at his big strong arms and his sexy ass goatee. He was always well dressed and groomed. She was hoping they went somewhere they could be alone just the two of them. She wanted to get to know him personally.

She knew the story behind him going to jail. She didn't care about his past. She believe in people changing. It's been two weeks since Desmond been gone and LOC was bored out this mind. He wanted this date to be perfect. He was really interested in Tracey and he wanted to be faithful to her. Tracey was marriage material; she didn't have any kids of her own. When LOC told Tracey to get sexy for him, she did just that. When he arrived to pick her up from her house he didn't blow he got out and knocked on the door. She answered the door wearing a long laced see through fitted dress, her hair was pinned up into a bun and her makeup was flawless. He looked down at her feet and noticed she had beautiful feet. He didn't care about her heels. She was always wearing jeans or joggers he didn't even notice she had a body. She had hips and curves out of this world. He gave her a dozen of white roses. She thought that was very nice of him. He wasn't dressed in a suit but he had on a nice pair of jeans with a polo shirt and a pair of Jordan's on. He still had to keep it gangsta. His chain cost about 10 racks. It was iced out with blue and yellow diamonds. His yellow 10 karat pinky ring cost damn near what he paid for the chain. He had on some blue and yellow 3 karat diamond earrings in both ears. He was looking good as hell to Tracey.

She was looking good as hell to him too. He told Tracey he thought she would look sexier getting out the truck than she would the car. Tracey had never road with no one with big tires and rims before. It was a turn on a lil bit. He decided to take Tracey to a restaurant right off the shore. So they could see the waves from the beach water while they ate, talked and got to know each other more. They opened up about how they felt about one another. LOC was shocked to hear Tracey said she had been interested in him the whole time. She barely said two words to him at the funeral. After dinner Tracey wanted to walk out by the beach so her feet could feel the sand and water. LOC had never been on a date like this but he was digging it. They walked along the beach and held hands as they walked and talked. He was really enjoying her company and she was enjoying his too.

After spending a few hours together and getting to know one another LOC took Tracey back home he gave her a hug and a kiss on her cheek and told her goodnight. When Tracey got behind her closed doors she wanted to scream. Just thinking about how good he smelled and how handsome he was looking. He was taking it slow with her so he wasn't gone rush into anything. She was thinking about cooking dinner and inviting him over so he wouldn't have to feel like he always had to take her out. Two weeks had passed and Talonda nor LOC has heard anything from Desmond. Talonda was starting to worry. She sent him a letter but he never responded. She called to the county jail to see if he was transferred there. But he wasn't there. He was still in juvenile lockup. Talonda called over to the juvenile jail to check on her baby, but they wouldn't give her any information. She thought he would have had a court date by now. They wouldn't give her any information on what's going on with Desmond or tell her when he will have a court date.

Talonda called LOC worrying because she didn't know what to do. LOC didn't really have no connections with the juvenile side. He told Talonda not to stress, if something bad happen they would call her. Talonda just needed to talk to her son. Desmond was giving one phone call after he was booked, but he refused to use his call. Desmond didn't want to speak to no one on the outside for a while. He was trying to concentrate on what he wanted to do with his life when his case was over. He would never get over the fact he killed his brother. That hole in his heart will never heal. He only had 40 racks saved up, but he knew his mom wasn't working and eventually she was gone need some money to help pay the bills. Talonda didn't know he put away 40 racks in Shelley's account. He left 10 racks at the house. He didn't tell nobody the money was there. He left the money there so the closer it got for school to start, his mom would be able to get the kids what they need. He hid 5 racks in one spot and 5 in another spot. He wasn't fully ready to trust his mom with that much money. He knew she was going through a lot and he knew she could eventually slip back into her old ways. Desmond wasn't communicating with his mom on purpose. He was testing her strength to see if she was gone keep her word about staying clean.

He wanted to call her but he knew she would be waiting by the phone for him to call. Krystal reached out to him, he was happy but yet surprised to hear from her. He just knew she wasn't gone have shit else to say to him after she heard what he was locked up for. Desmond didn't have a clue he had made the paper. Krystal wrote him and told him she read the article about him in the paper, and she read the article about DJ in the paper also. She thought it was very brave of him to turn his self in. She told Desmond she knows he's not a bad person she had been watching him more than he thought. She was giving Desmond hope, her words of inspiration made him stronger. Just by her telling him she would be there for him as long he don't get out and give her his ass to kiss. Krystal really liked Desmond and they barely had the chance to talk or kick it and she was still willing to be there for him as much as she could. Desmond had Krystal going down to his mother's house to see Shelly just so he can find out if his mom was doing right and not back out there in the streets. He didn't want Krystal to even mention to Shelly that she had been communicating with him by mail.

Shelly would have started crying and she would have told their mom. Desmond didn't know anything about his case or what they was gone do all he knew was he was just sitting in there. It was people coming in and going to court the next day. He hadn't talked to nobody. In the meantime Krystal was writing him and sending him pics trying to keep him level headed. Desmond was starting to think the worse, people were getting visits, and they never mentioned to him about a visit. He would have loved to see Krystal but its only immediate family that could visit. The first few nights was rough for him. He was having constant nightmares about DJ. In every dream DJ was smiling and laughing like he did when he was alive. All the beef they had between one another when they was on the streets together never popped up in his dream. They were all good dreams and they made him think about what his mom had told him.

He wanted to write LOC but he didn't want them to have that address on file. He didn't want to lead to police in no direction they didn't have a clue about. He thought he could use the phones whenever he wanted too, if he had money. Juvenile was different from what he saw on TV. He couldn't call and he didn't use money in there. They state and tax payers paid for everything he was going to need. He received a letter from his auntie Tracey he was happy to hear from her. She told him about her date with LOC and how much she was starting to like him. She told Desmond he treats her like a woman is supposed to be treated. She also wanted to know why he hasn't responded to his mom letters or called her. Tracey knew Desmond would respond to her. Desmond had a way to contact LOC now. LOC was the one person that could talk to him and calm him down, especially when it came to him stressing about his case.

He wrote his aunt Tracey back and told her he was holding up pretty good, and he didn't want them to worry about him. He hadn't wrote his mom back because he was trying to see if she would use that as an excuse to go back in the streets. Talonda had been doing so well. She promised Desmond she was done with the streets and she hadn't been back out there. She's been going to her meetings on a regular. Her counselors is still active in her life and there for her while she's still going through her grieving process. When Tracey let Desmond know that his mom kept her word and she's doing everything she could to stay on the right track for herself and for them. She told him he needs to reach out to her because she has enough on her heart. She have sleepless nights since he's been gone because she's been worried about him.

After the conversation Talonda had with LOC he didn't think for once she would go back out there. Talonda had never broke down to no one before but she told LOC everything. It made her feel so much better to get it off her chest. She wanted a clean slate. She was on the urge of getting her another job with the job placement program through the sobriety home. She had started fixing herself up every day like she use too. Talonda knew she had to eventually get a job, it was no one left that would help her pay bills like Desmond and DJ did. She had to complete her 90 days with the sobriety house before they would help her find a job. In the mean time she was cool because other agencies were helping since she lost her son. It's been three weeks since Desmond has been locked up. He finally called his mom. She was so happy to hear his voice. She asked him why haven't he called or responded.

He didn't tell her because he was testing her strength. He told her he was trying to adjust and not think about what's going on the outside because he would be there for a very long time. Talonda told Desmond not to think that way. She believes that he will come home soon. It all sounded good to Desmond but he focused on the bigger picture. The fact he was locked up for murder. He was young but he knew you didn't just get a slap on the wrist for murder. Talonda advised Desmond of all the people that said they would be a witness for him. Once again it all sound good hearing it, but it's totally different when it's time to come speak up. Desmond was listening to a few dudes that was in there talk about how they family don't come and see them and how they can't go home because their moms won't come to court. Desmond knew that no matter how high his mom was if one of them or both of them was locked up, and his aunt Tracey found out. She was going to make sure his mom showed up for court.

Desmond was listening to the petty reasons why they were locked up and he like damn you in here for bullshit like pissing outside and loitering. One nigga named Man Man was in there for burglary. The other nigga name was Roy he was locked up for selling drugs and stealing cars. He even had a couple of kids already. Roy mom was on drugs, that's why Roy had to get out and get it on his own at an early age too. He had problems similar to Desmond's. He turned eighteen, he was around DJ's age but they still had him locked up in the juvenile jail. He was fucking with an older bitch. He and Desmond got along pretty good. He kind of reminded Desmond of DJ. Desmond didn't want nobody to know about his charges, but they found out anyways. He didn't want people to be scared of him. He definitely didn't want no rank for killing his bro. He didn't talk about it too much and Roy didn't ask too many questions. When it comes to jail you just don't ask a lot of questions.

It makes you look like a snitch. If and when Desmond wanted to talk about it then Roy would find out. Roy was fucking with him a bitch that was a lil older than he was. She was like four years older than he was. Kind of like DJ Tootie's situation. Only difference is that Tootie didn't have kids and she was a lot older than DJ. It seemed like everything was starting to remind him of DJ. He would often sit in his room and DJ would come sit on the bed next to him to let him know he was still there. Roy knew Desmond was dealing with some mental issues because he would sit in his room for hours. Other dudes would joke about it, saying he like sitting in his room so he could beat his meat. Some days Desmond would wake up with bags under his eyes from not sleeping. The more days that went by and he didn't hear anything the more he was getting stressed. Roy reached out to Desmond and told him if he ever needed to talk he would be there for him. Desmond just shook his head as if he was agreeing with Roy. Him and Roy was alright but he wasn't about to trust nann other nigga. His own niggas was turning on him, his own brother turned on him and tried to kill him. Shiddd Desmond was gone keep his guards up at all times.

Especially in the joint, he knew it wasn't nothing but snake ass niggas in there. The only nigga he trusted was himself while he was locked up. The only nigga he trusted on the streets was LOC. Man Man on the other hand never took his charges or anything else serious. He thought everything was a joke til he went to court and found out he was about to get sent to placement. That's when shit got real for him. He was always used to his mom showing up for court, and he get sent home on house arrest or probation. Now he was about to be sent somewhere he didn't have a clue about. Desmond was thinking they would probably do the same thing to him and he wouldn't be able to see his family for a very long time. Three months has passed and finally Desmond was brought into the interrogation room and questioned by the detective that was over the case. When he saw the word interrogation he thought they were going to do him like they did the people on TV.

He thought they would throw him up against the walls; sling chairs at him and slam him on tables. Desmond didn't want to relive that day, but he knew he would have too every time he went to court or talked to any detective. He worked his self up for no reason at all. The detective just wanted him to tell him his recollection of what happened on the night DJ was killed again. Desmond started from the beginning and told him every single detail that lead up to DJ's murder. The more Desmond talked about it, the more he was starting to break down. That was his first time breaking down since he was taken into custody. He couldn't tell if the detective was believing his story or not. He didn't show no emotion. He didn't try to console Desmond or anything. He treated him as if he was really a murderer. Desmond didn't want sympathy but he didn't want people to believe he did it on purpose. Once the detective finished with him, he just took him back to his section. He didn't tell him when he was going to court, or what he was actually charged with. He didn't know anything.

People was coming and leaving the next day, he was just there. He finally wrote his mom and asked her to come and visit him. After all he's been there 3 months and she still been doing well. He wanted her to come and visit him so he could tell her how proud he was of her. He wanted to see Krystal he was starting to think about her a lot. To get his mind off everything else. Krystal had found her a part-time job while she was in school, so she didn't write him as much. Desmond thought she probably got her a new nigga, but that wasn't the case. Krystal was feeling the shit outta Desmond. She was willing to ride it out with him as long as she could. Krystal wanted Desmond to be in a committed relationship with her. Desmond felt like she was the only person with freedom that could cheat. But then again he remembered how LOC said he use to get pussy in jail from the C.O.'s. Desmond didn't want to get too wrapped up into Krystal and she hurt him.

He took everything one day at a time. Krystal was still a virgin at least that's what she told him. She wanted to lose her virginity to him. Krystal been wanting Desmond for so long and now that she has the chance to have him, she refused to let him go. She couldn't wait til she could go visit him. Desmond would call and talk to her whenever he would get a phone call privilege. Since she started working at the mall, he couldn't talk to her. In the meantime he would call his mom and talk to her. Shelly was missing Desmond every day. She wanted him to be at home with them so bad. Even though DJ and Dre was dead she still didn't feel safe being at home. She was scared to walk to the candy store. She would just sit out in the front with her siblings and let them play. Krystal would come and talk to her on her off days sometimes. Shelly and her mom was starting to build up a mother and daughter relationship. They would cook together and watch family movies together.

Talonda asked Krystal if she could help her get a job at the store she worked at in the mall. Krystal was all for it. Anything to support Desmond. Talonda went and applied at the clothing store Krystal works at. Krystal talked to the hiring manager for Talonda and two weeks later Talonda was called in for an interview. She was hired the same day. Talonda was nervous but excited at the same time. She hadn't worked in sum years but she was ready to do what she had to do. Talonda was afraid that her old boss would give her a bad reference. So she used the people from the treatment center as references. They was very proud of Talonda for getting her a job and trying to better herself. Everyone was proud of Talonda for getting herself together. She couldn't wait for Desmond to find out she knew he would be so proud of her. It would definitely earn Krystal some cool point with him also.

Talonda really respected Krystal for being there for Desmond. Krystal would come sit over at Talonda's house when she was off so Shelly wouldn't be there by herself. Moma Tanya met Krystal and instantly started to like her. When Desmond found out how Krystal was getting along with his family and how she looked out for his mom. He started praying and asking GOD for another chance. He really didn't want to lose Krystal. She was like the best thing that has happened to him since he caught his case. Talonda felt good about herself getting up getting dressed, combing her hair and putting on make-up going to work. She didn't have a car, so she would either catch the bus or ride with Krystal if they worked on the same days. Talonda knew it was gone be a challenge trying to get back on her feet, but she was up for the challenge. She was starting to care of business like a mother supposed to. Her caseworker helped her get childcare for the younger children so the older ones could do afterschool activities and get involved into other things. Talonda was even going in on her off days so she would be able to provide everything the kids needed. She worked her job for six months and was doing so good.

He mom bought her a brand new Suburban so she would have transportation for her and the kids. When Moma Tanya took Talonda to pick out her truck. Talonda didn't know how to express her gratitude to her mom. She was beyond happy; she never knew that her life would be coming together so quickly. She felt like the devil was attacking her and her family constantly. Moma Tanya paid the notes for her and Tracey volunteered to pay the insurance until Talonda got on her feet. The store manager offered Talonda a manager's position since she had been doing so well and she knew the ends about running the store. Krystal was still in high school so she couldn't take the position. She was happy to know they offered it to Talonda.

Krystal didn't know everything that Talonda been through as far as her addiction but she knew some things from talking to Desmond. Desmond was never the type of person to tell his business less long family business. He only talked to LOC when he had problems he couldn't figure out on his own. Nine months and two weeks have gone by and Desmond still hasn't went to court or anything. He was started to get a lil depressed because he was just sitting there and not knowing what was going on. He wanted to go to court because at least he would know what kind of time he's looking at. He was gone try to chill and not stress about it. He knew the longer he sat that time would be counted as good time. He started playing basketball so he could keep his mind off everything that was going on in the real world.

Chapter 11

An entire year has passed and Desmond finally received his court date. It was a bitter sweet moment for him, because his court date was on DJ's 19th birthday. Desmond was fucked up over it too. He thought they did that shit on purpose to him. He thought they were trying to send the judge mixed signals by scheduling his court date like that. When he went into court he was happy to see his mom, Shelly, Krystal, LOC and his aunt Tracey. Only immediate family was allowed to go in juvenile court so Talonda said Krystal was his Desmond's sister and LOC was his uncle. Desmond was excited to hear what his outcome was gone be but all they did was read him his charges and reschedule the court date 30 from that day. He was a lil happy to see them but he was pissed that he had to wait another 30 days to see what his fate was gone be. Krystal made sure she was looking damn good when she went to court.

She was trying to give Desmond something to think about for a while. She made sure her jeans were nice and fitted so her ass could look real plumped and round. Desmond was trying to get a good look at her but Shelly was too busy blowing Desmond kisses and yelling out she loves him as the bailiff walked him away in handcuffs. It broke Talonda's heart to see her son being handcuffed like a caged animal. Tracey tried to be strong for Talonda and not cry as she watched her nephew being led away by the guard. When Desmond got back to his section he held his composer, so the other dudes wouldn't see him getting soft. He was happy as hell to see Krystal right there though. He didn't now she was even coming. She surprised him with that one. He was really starting to believe that Krystal would be there for him. Talonda thought she would be able to at least hug her son, but juveniles get treated just like a regular prisoner. While they were leaving Talonda spotted one of the prosecutors that was in the courtroom and she asked him if he knew about how much time Desmond was facing.

The prosecutor told Talonda he didn't know as of yet, they were still investigating. Talonda told him that her son admitted to everything so what's the investigation about. The prosecutor then told her that they were investigating if it was self-defense or not. They were still talking to witnesses. He wouldn't give out any information on the witnesses or who they were to protect them from retaliation of sum sort. Desmond tried not to focus on how bad the outcome could be. He just focused on what he was going to do if he ever saw the streets again. Roy was about to get transferred to the county the next day. He told Desmond he would stay in contact with him because they built a good friendship in jail. Roy didn't know his fate at the time. He and Desmond couldn't communicate while Desmond was in Juvenile. They switched information so they could keep in contact upon their release date or whomever gets out first. Desmond knew Roy would touch down before he did. When Roy left the next day

Desmond really didn't have no one to talk too, so he spent his free time working out. He attended school while he was locked up to get the knowledge he was gone need to become a rap artist. He started going to the library to get information on self-defense cases. All he wanted was another chance at freedom so he can do the right thing with his life. Desmond would start writing rhymes to get his mind off of shit. He started putting his thoughts and anger into music. All the new comers thought he was weird because he would walk around rapping a few of his lyrics, but they thought he was talking to himself. Everyone that came in obviously found out he was in there for murder. He was the only kid locked up on a very serious charge. Desmond didn't care or focus on what they said about him, he was trying to free his mind of all the bullshit and drama that was going on in his life. Desmond was approaching 18. He didn't know if they were going to send him to the county or keep him in juvenile. He wanted to ask his counselor but he thought they would think he cared more about getting out than killing his brother.

Desmond didn't want to be a problem for none of the guards. He was trying to do everything right so when he did get the day in court he had been waiting for they would give a good behavior report on him. Desmond felt like he couldn't win for losing his court was scheduled 30 from his last court date and they rescheduled it. Now he has court in the same week as his birthday. He went to court on DJ's birthday now he has to go to court the day before his birthday. He felt like the devil was attacking him. Out of all the good he has ever done in his life he felt like nothing was on his side. He knew selling drugs was wrong but he was tryna provide for his family. He felt like what was a man supposed to do. Although he was just a child he had responsibilities of a man. Once again he felt like giving up. He was able to call his mom and talk to her for 5 minutes. He told her that he didn't think he had the courage to fight that case. Talonda told him to just keep praying GOD gives the strongest battles to his servants. Desmond didn't know what that meant.

Moma Tanya was over Talonda's house and she was able to talk to Desmond for the first time since he had been locked up. She prayed for him on the phone and told him she loves him and she will be waiting for him to get released. After his granny prayed for him, he took that anger and put it into his music. He found that putting his anger and frustrations into music relieved him of stress. The more he wrote the more he started feeling like he was being freed from everything. In the middle of the night he would get up and start writing whenever lyrics came into his head. All Desmond would do is work out and write. His entire demeanor changed day to day. Krystal was keeping him motivated and being there for him like she said she would. Desmond was starting to become a different person and he could feel the difference. At his next court date he was told that he would be charged as an adult and they would charge him with manslaughter instead of capital murder. With the manslaughter charge he was facing 10 to 15.

That fucked his head all up because he thought he was gone definitely walk up outta there. At that very moment he knew shit was about to get real he just didn't know when. For once he didn't break down he took what the judge said and went back to his room and put it into music. Talonda broke down in court but Desmond refused to drop another tear. He waited for the time for them to take him over to the county. He figured the least time he could do was 5 and the most was 10. Either way he was ready to get the shit over with. Desmond sat in juvenile lock up for three more months. The day came for him to be transferred to the county. He thought he would see Roy in the county but he was transferred to D.O.C to complete his time. He only had a year left to do then he would be a free man. Desmond didn't know when he was going to prison but he knew he had to make the best of his situation wherever he goes including in the county. Desmond saw a few niggas from the hood and one of the niggas that was out there when he shot DJ.

It was cool to him having a few dudes from the hood up in there, but Desmond ain't wanna fuck with nobody. He just wanted to do his time and get out dat bitch. He was able to use the phone whenever he wanted too now. He called his mom collect and told her he was in the county so they could put some money on his books. He called his aunt Tracey because he knew she was gone look out. When he called Tracey she was chilling with LOC and he was happy to talk to LOC. Desmond asked LOC if he and Tracey could take Shelley to the bank so she could get sum money to put on his books. LOC told Desmond don't worry about no money we got you lil nigga. Desmond was just tryna get enough money on his books so he didn't have to ask a motherfucker for shit. He didn't want shit from the cats he knew in there either. He wanted his own shit. LOC gave Tracey $200 and told her to go put that on Desmond's books. He made sure Desmond had $200 on his books every two weeks.

He knew of all people what it was like to be locked up with nothing. LOC reached out to the C.O. he knew that worked in the county and asked her to look out for him and make sure he was straight til his money hit his books. When niggas found out he was cool with LOC and Dead Eye they was showing him hella love. Desmond wanted to put that part of his life behind him, but he knew he needed that love shown. He was more respected than he thought he would be. He knew Dead Eye and LOC had clout but he didn't know they had it like that. They didn't have any enemies because niggas was scared of them. LOC wasn't the aggressive one Dead Eye was. LOC humbled himself a lot since he got out of prison, but people knew how he was before. After Dead Eye loss his moms he didn't give a fuck about shit not even his own life. Dead Eye even had one of his bitches to put $200 on Desmond books for him. Krystal didn't have much but she sent him $50 every two weeks. Talonda didn't have to do shit but go to work and focus on her and the kids.

No matter how Desmond felt about Dead Eye fucking his mother, he still looked out for him like he always has. Dead Eye did sum fucked up shit on his own but he was still loyal when it came to looking out for one another. Desmond thought no matter what that's how he and DJ would have been. Desmond blocked the entire DJ situation out his head. He knew it wouldn't bring him back. He needed to focus on the future and not the past. Desmond didn't want no visits for the first couple of weeks he wanted to adjust. He couldn't see Krystal for three more months because she wasn't eighteen yet. He knew Shelly was dying to see him, but he wanted to prepare himself mentally because he knew she would start crying once she saw him. As time prevailed

Desmond continued to focus on his music and continued to work out. Talonda and the kids would go and visit him weekly, not giving no one else time to go and see him. Tracey wanted to go but Talonda wanted to see him as much as she could before he got shipped off somewhere far. Tracey didn't want to complain but she took care of Desmond like he was her own son as well. Ninety days has passed and he was still sitting in the county, but he was able to start getting visits from Krystal. He couldn't wait to put her down on his visitation list. During his entire stay in jail Krystal has been very supportive of him. Desmond knew 5-10 years was gone be a long time for Krystle to wait for him and he couldn't blame her if she had left him. He fucked up his own life and he didn't want to hold her back. He wanted to tell her that she could just move on with her life but every time he would she would cut him off and tell him she's gonna wait for him. It sounded good but he knew every day was a different day. He knew eventually she was gone want to start fucking and want the feeling of being hugged up with a nigga. She would go and see him once a week either before his mom or after his mom. She made the time pass quickly to him.

He enjoyed every visit they spent together while it lasted. He would daze into her pretty brown eyes and dream about kissing her full sized lips. Krystal made him feel so good on the inside and she didn't even know it. He made her feel good too. She imagined her life with Desmond long before he knew she had a crush on him. After six months had passed. Desmond knew his time was narrowing down to be at the county. He knew once he wasn't able to see Krystal like he wanted too, everything was gone change. He was really feeling her, but he knew he was gone have to fall back. He started telling her not to put money on his books and started refusing some of her visits. He was breaking her heart and he didn't want too but he knew it was better for the both of them. Krystal would be at work crying and asking Talonda why is he treating her like that. Talonda didn't have the answers Krystal was looking for.

Talonda waited to hear from Desmond and asked him why he was treating Krystal like that. He told his mom that he couldn't be a good friend or boyfriend to her while he's locked up. He didn't want her to put her life on hold for him. Desmond knew anything could happen in jail and he could end up with more time, he wanted Krystal to have a good life. She was a good girl and she deserved to have a good life. He knew if he was out on the streets still, she wouldn't have to worry about shit. She showed her loyalty to him just by being there for him while he's locked up. As much as he said he was putting the DJ situation behind him. It was certain things like how Krystal acted toward him that made him think about DJ. When DJ was with Tootie or them other bitches they didn't have his back like he thought they did. He wish DJ had found him one chick that was like Krystal. Desmond wrote 20 songs since he has started working on his music. He has never mentioned to none of his family or Krystal about him writing music. Krystal could tell he was working out because his body was starting to look good as hell to her.

Krystal went from talking to Desmond every other day to maybe once a week. He would call his mom and Aunt Tracey but he fell back off of calling Krystal. Talonda tried talking to him and letting him know he was hurting her, but she understood his point. She told Krystal that Desmond is just going through sum things mentally and this entire transition was getting the best of him. Krystal understood what Talonda was saying but she wanted him to know that no matter what she was gone be there for him. Krystal knew he listens to LOC and he looks up to him. She knew it would be hard to get in contact with LOC without anyone knowing. She would see him at the mall sometimes, but now that she's looking for him she never sees him. Krystal planned such a beautiful life with Desmond. He was all she ever wanted. After doing nine months in the county Desmond was transferred to D.O.C. No one knew Desmond was going to be transferred, he didn't know.

He was woke up at 4 in the morning and told to get his belongings together. This was when he knew shit was about to get real. He was taken to an inmate processing center for thirty days. Desmond didn't know where he was going but he knew that the ride to get there was long as hell. Especially to be handcuffed to other niggas. After riding for three long hours and only stopping for one restroom break. It wasn't anything like the county. He never felt violated before in his life. They looked at his entire body and he was checked for illnesses and diseases. He couldn't use the phone there he could only write and receive letters. That was the only time Desmond was ready to go to where he was gone do his time at. They were very strict and all he could do was work out to pass the time.

He only was allowed two sheets of paper a week so he had to choose who he wanted to write. He wrote his mom so she could know where he was at. He didn't write Krystal at all to tell her. After his thirty days he was on his way to his destination. He was sent all the way to Brickell Department of Correction five hours away from home. He had never heard of that prison before. He knew they housed a lot of inmates because the prison was big as hell. He sat in holding for about two days waiting to get processed. He often wondered if they had sent Roy to the same prison because he hadn't spoken to him. Desmond didn't know anybody at that prison and that wasn't the same prison LOC had did his time at. Desmond contacted his mom so she could set up a payment account so they would know how to put money on his books. Desmond sat in jail two weeks waiting for them to send over all the money he had on his books from the county.

Finally after being there for three weeks LOC sent him another $200. Desmond wasn't worried about the money problems he was more worried about them niggas trying to pull sum bullshit because he didn't know anybody in there. He was with some other murders and bigger drug dealers. He was locked up with niggas that will never see the streets again. All he could think about was the shit that happened to dudes in prison on TV. He made up in his mind that he wasn't going out like no bitch. That was the only time he felt like if he had too he would kill again. While he was trying to adjust he remembered LOC telling him that he couldn't trust everybody in jail and not to show them niggas he was scared even if he was. He stayed mutual and continued to work on his music and work out. He kept going to the law library and taking different classes the prison offered to get time cuts off his possibly 15 year sentence. The time cuts wasn't much but three months. Any time cut off a nigga sentence made his feel an inch closer to coming home. He signed up for the GED program, but he couldn't get into that class until the following year.

He wasn't tripping because he knew he wasn't going anywhere. It would knock six month off his sentence and put him at step closer to parole. So far Desmond had had good behavior in jail and they decided to put him in a lower level lock up. He was pretty cool until he found out he was locked up with child molesters and rapists. He hated those type of motherfuckers. He blamed them for him being locked up. Although they had nothing to do with him. He felt like if DJ hadn't of never did what he done to Shelly he wouldn't be in jail. He never communicated with none of them or sat at the table with them at chow time. Desmond refused to be around them. While he was in jail he received a letter from Roy. He thought Roy forgotten about him because he hadn't heard nothing from him. He thought Roy was still locked up but he saw the return address on the envelope. Roy was telling him to keep his head up and he will stay in contact with him.

Roy told Desmond once he was released he would touch down on him so they could chop shit up. Desmond wrote Roy every blu moon, because he wasn't about to be writing no nigga constantly from jail like he was his bitch. Roy was a cool dude and all but Desmond knew dat nigga was a thief that nigga stole cars and would take them to the scrap yards for money. He knew he couldn't bring Roy around Dead Eye and LOC because they didn't fuck with too many niggas. If they knew that nigga was a thief they would kill his ass themselves and probably him too for bringing him around. Desmond received a letter from Krystal. She was pouring her heart out to him. He didn't read her entire letter because it was making him feel weak. He wasn't tryna feel weak in there. He gave her the cold shoulder and never responded.

Krystal continue to be close with Talonda and Desmond's family while he was playing her shady. When Desmond sent his mom some visitation slips Krystle took one without Talonda knowing and filled it out and sent it in. She was determined to go and see Desmond rather he wanted her to or not. Once her visitation form was approved Desmond didn't trip because he knew it was too far for her to come and she didn't have a car. Desmond just let her feel like she was doing something by sending it in. He thought his mom gave it to her to fill out but he didn't ask to find out. Desmond sat in jail and focused on his time. He got to the point if they came to visit him he was okay with it if they didn't that was cool too.

Chapter 12

Tammy was dating a dude named Roy. He did a total of 3 years in jail in years in jail for auto theft and selling drugs. He called himself selling drugs but he would nickel and dime it every day. He didn't have a lot of money but the bitches liked him because he was nice looking. Tammy knew he was too young for her but he knew how to please her sexually. Tammy couldn't help she was a nympho. She loved to fuck but Roy wasn't giving it to her like she wanted it. He was too busy fucking all them lil nasty bitches that hang out at the court. He only fucked with bitches that had their own crib and car so he could use them for it. He never kept a job; he would always come up with an excuse why he couldn't work. He wanted to live the fast easy life but the quicker he made the money the quicker he spent it. Tammy loved him but she was getting tired of him using her car every day and never putting gas in it.

When it needed to be fixed he never had the money to fix it. Her mom and friends always told her she could do better, but she had faith in him. Whenever Tammy food stamps got on her card he would eat up her and her kid's food and never put food in the house when they were low. Her friends tried telling that Roy was only using her and that he was fucking with other bitches behind her back but she didn't listen. They would see Roy with other bitches in her car but every time they would tell her she would make up excuses and say that they were probably a

123

cousins or somebody. Tammy was very naïve when it came to Roy. She was putting up with shit from him that she didn't take off her kid's daddy. Whenever she would get paid all her money went toward the bills and Roy didn't help pay shit.

Every chance he had he would buy weed and when he would end up broke he would beg Tammy for money to get back on. He would tell Tammy he was sending his homeboy Desmond money in jail. During their entire relationship she has never heard of that dude before. When she wouldn't give it to him he would steal the lil money she had. She would always tell her friends about the things he would do to her. But whenever they would voice their opinion she would get mad and try to defend him. It gotten to the point they didn't even want to hear nothing about him when Tammy would bring him up. None of them liked him because how he treated her like pure shit, but she tried to convince them that he was really a good dude. When Tammy met Roy he had only two kids. She never saw his kids because he said he wasn't allowed to see them. Roy didn't take care of neither of his children to her knowledge. He was put on child support but because he didn't have a job so he couldn't pay shit.

He claimed that when he did get a lil job once child support took money from his check he would quit his job. She never saw any proof of that either. Tammy ex-boyfriend didn't want that nigga around his kids because he knew he was using her. Tammy just thought he was jealous because she was with somebody else. Her mother stopped helping her as long as she was with him because the kids would tell their grandmother how he was calling their mom out her name and get mad when she didn't give him money. Everybody could see he was a problem but Tammy. Even though Tammy was fucking a dude name Dead Eye before Roy came home. It was something about Roy she couldn't let go of. Dead Eye wasn't trying to be with her, he just wanted her to satisfy him. She did things with Dead Eye that she wouldn't dare do with Roy. If Dead Eye wanted her to be his girl she would have. She would've left Roy for him. For sum reason she loved them young immature ass niggas.

She loved Roy more than she loved herself. She just loved the way Dead Eye dicked her down. It was times when Roy would leave her stranded in her own car at work. She would have to pay the daycare lady late fees because he wouldn't bring her car back on time so she could pick up her kids on time. Roy didn't give a fuck about Tammy nor her kids, hell he didn't care about his own damn kids. Tammy went to the club with her girls and a female approached her and asked her if she was fucking with Roy, Tammy told her, "yeah." and she told Tammy, "I fucks with him too and if that's your car he be driving, I be driving it too." "What the fuck you mean you be driving my car?" Asked Tammy. She told Tammy "well he don't have license so I was driving so he won't get pulled over and go to jail?" Tammy girl Mona looked at her and asked, "So is you gone let that shit ride?" Tammy responded with a soft voice and said, "Well she was doing me a favor and preventing from getting my car towed."

Mona looked at Tammy and said, "you got to be the stupidest bitch I know!" "I wish another bitch would tell me she was driving my shit while my nigga had it!" Tammy had a stupid look on her face she tried to justify it to Mona but she wasn't trying to hear shit she was saying. The following day Roy was gone all day and night in Tammy's car. After the bitch told her she be driving her shit. She still let him take her car. He wouldn't answer her phone calls or shit. He knew she had to take the kids to school and to daycare, but he still didn't give a fuck. Tammy called Roy back to back, she texted him and told him she needed to get the kids to school, and he finally texted her back and told her to catch the bus to take them. Tammy texted him back and said, why should she have to catch the bus and I have a car. He didn't respond back to her text. She knew that if she called Mona she was gone talk shit to her.

So she decided to call Leslie because she very seldom commented on anything that had to do with Roy and her situation. Leslie got up and took Tammy to drop the kids off and took Tammy to work. Tammy kept calling Roy but he still wasn't returning any of her phone calls. On Leslie way back home she stopped at the gas station to get sum gas. She happens to see Roy pull up with another bitch in Tammy's car. Leslie went and confronted Roy herself, she wasn't quick to jump on the phone and call Tammy. Leslie told Roy she knows he's grown and he can fuck with whomever he like, but she know her girl really do love him. Cuz if she didn't she wouldn't be putting up with his shit. But if he gone keep playing her like an ass he needs to just leave her the fuck alone. Roy told Leslie "I'm a grown ass man and I do what the fuck I wanna do!" "Tammy is my bitch, she already know what's up!" "She knew I didn't want to be in no committed relationship when she started fucking with me". Leslie said "well I don't appreciate having to get out of my bed to take the kids to school and to daycare plus drop her off at work and she has her own damn car!" Roy responded and said, "You did it because you wanted too!" "I told the bitch to catch the damn bus!" Leslie just shook her head at Roy and finished pumping her gas and drove off.

She made sure she said everything loud enough so the chick in the car could hear their conversation and see what type of nigga he really is. As Leslie got ready to drive off she noticed Roy and the chick was looking at her smiling as if they were talking about her. Leslie called Mona and told her what had just happened. Mona told Leslie, "I don't give a fuck anymore because Tammy was gone keep putting up with his shit anyways!" Leslie agreed with Tammy and said she wasn't gone keep getting out of her bed to take her to work and drop the kids off if she was gone still be letting him take her car. Mona told Leslie, "Roy sometimes take Tammy's car while she's sleep." Tammy doesn't even know he gone in her car until she gets up the next morning. Leslie said "well her dumb ass needs to start hiding her keys." Mona said, "Fuck hiding her keys she needs to put his ass out like both of his baby mama's did when they got tired of his shit." "She don't even have kids with his ass and she's taking his shit off him."

Leslie told Mona, "Tammy was fucking another nigga while he was locked up, so she can't understand why she is being stupid for him." Mona said, "That's why I don't be wanting to hear that shit no mo when she be coming to me with it." "She knew not to call me and ask for no damn ride, cuz I already told her ass." Tammy called Leslie when it was time for her to get off work because she needed a ride. Leslie asked, "Did you call Roy?" Tammy said, "yeah but he's not answering." Leslie replied, "I'm gone come get yo ass this last time but if you keep letting Roy fuck over you then I'm not helping you anymore. Tammy said, "But you supposed to be my girl." Leslie said, "I am your girl, that's why it pisses me off to see you put up with his shit." "You ain't never put up with shit like this." "When you was with Damein the minute you found out he was cheating you left him alone." "We be telling you we see Roy with bitches in yo car and you try to justify the bullshit each and every time." "By the way, I saw him at the gas station after I dropped you off with a bitch in your car once again now justify the shit for him this time too."

Tammy asked Leslie, "Describe the girl." Leslie said, "for what Tammy it ain't gone mean shit." Tammy started crying her eyes out to Leslie telling her, "I can't understand why he treats me this way, because I'm nothing but good to him." Leslie said, "maybe because he don't love you he just love the fact he can control your car and get whatever the fuck he want from you." Leslie said, "Tammy he don't have his own shit, if you put him out he gone go to the next bitch or right back to his mama house." "He barely have money when he gets broke he runs to you." "He don't put gas in your car." "Why do you need him and you doing well all by yourself?" Tammy knew everything Leslie was saying was the truth. Leslie told her "your own mother won't talk to you because you letting him take advantage of you." Tammy said "my mother don't like nobody I be with."

Leslie said, "but she started respecting Damein because he did take care of you and his kids and the one that ain't his." "Terrell don't even come by to see his son." "All yo kids call Damein daddy, and that's fucked up because he only has two by you." "Roy don't have none and you be making them call him daddy." "Why would you have them calling him daddy and he doesn't fuck with his own kids?" Tammy responded and said, "I all of a sudden became naïve I guess." Leslie laughed and said, "naïve no bitch you became stupid ass hell!" They had to change the conversation because they were picking up the kids and Leslie doesn't talk about grown up shit in front of the kids. When Tammy' oldest boy Lil Terrell got in the car he told his mom he heard Roy on the phone asking somebody do they love and miss him. Leslie looked at Tammy and rolled her eyes and shook her head at the same time. Tammy really felt like shit to hear her son say that but is that enough for her to leave him alone, nope because she was laying up with him that same night after her didn't show up to take her to work or to pick her up.

The kids liked being at their grandmothers house but Tammy didn't let them go over there because she thought her mom was questioning them about what goes on in her house. She would drill into her kids head what goes on in her house staying her house, but every chance they got they made sure they told their grandmother everything and also told her they didn't like Roy or liked him living with them. When Tammy parents divorced she had very little contact with her father, she was mad because he cheated on her mom and that lead to their divorce. When Tammy's mom had enough of the situation with Tammy and Roy she contacted Tammy's father and told him that he needed to talk some sense into his daughter.

Despite how Tammy felt about her father she knew he didn't take any shit off nobody especially a lil want to be thug nigga. Tammy knew her she was on the urge of losing her friends because they got tired of the situation and wanted nothing else to do with Roy and Tammy's relationship. Tammy was off the next day after she dropped the kids off at school and daycare; she went to the grocery store. She was confronted in the store by a chick who said she was pregnant with Roy's baby. Tammy called Roy while she was in the store and asked him if she was pregnant by him and Roy denied knowing what Tammy was talking about. He told her "damn!" "I been out four months now I got a bitch pregnant!" "You stupid as fuck!" "That's why I be out all night because of your nagging ass!" "It's always something with you!" He instantly got an attitude with her, telling her, "You gets on my fucking nerves asking me stupid shit, that's why I don't like to be around you!" "You believe everything a bitch tell you!" He told Tammy, "You be stressing me out that's why I never come home!"

It never fails Tammy let him turn the tables on her like it was all her fault. He was the one doing all the shit and she apologizing to him. She told the chick "he said that wasn't his baby and she believes her man." The girl laughed at Tammy and said, "yo man yeah ok!" "If he was yo man why was he laid up with me when you were calling him for yo car to go to work, and he told you to catch the fucking bus with yo kids!" "I know yo girl told you she saw us together at the gas station in your car." Tammy really wanted to punch her ass but she knew if she did she would go to jail for hitting a pregnant girl. She was pissed off more at herself because she knew the bitch wasn't lying because how would she know he told her to catch the bus. Tammy knew she looked like a stupid ass in front of that girl, but she tried to play it off as best as she could. She told her "well when yo baby get here he will take a test to see if it's his." The girl told Tammy, "I'm not taking shit to prove a point to you and he know it's his he never said shit to me about no damn blood test." "But if he wanna act stupid I will make him look like a damn fool too." Tammy said "he don't take care of the kids he already got." She replied to Tammy "well why you with him then?" "Because he do for me when we together,"

Tammy replied and said "if you knew that's my car why did you get in it?" She said "no I didn't find out that was your car til I overheard yo girl talking to him." "He told me that was his car, hell I have driven the car before to get something to eat while he was at my house" It was one thing for Tammy's son to hear him talking to a bitch on the phone but it was another to have possibly have another bitch driving her car. Tammy decided to call Roy again to ask him did her have this bitch driving her car. When Roy answered the phone and Tammy asked him "did you have this same chick that says she pregnant by you driving my fucking car?" Roy hung up on her. The girl laughed at Tammy and said, "why is you tripping you gone still gone be fucking with that nigga?" Tammy said "but you fucking with him too." She replied to Tammy and said "Yup shole is!" "I'm gone fuck with him until I feel like I wanna stop." Tammy asked her "if you know we together why would you continue to fuck with him?" She said very nonchalant to Tammy "because I can and I will and ain't you or nobody else gone stop me!"

Tammy rolled her eyes and said "you just lucky you pregnant right now because if you weren't, I would mop this store wit yo ass!" The girl laughed as she walked off and said but "I won't be pregnant forever so whenever you ready just let me know!" Tammy didn't want to get loud in the store, she was so pissed she didn't get nothing she came to the store to get. Tammy knew Roy was lying and that girl was telling the fucking truth. She just didn't know what she wanted to do about the situation. Tammy's feelings was so hurt all she could do was sit in her car and cry her eyes out because she loved Roy a lot despite her fucking with Dead Eye. She didn't want to go home to face him and hear a bunch of lies so she went to Mona's house. She knew Mona was gone talk shit but she rather hear what Mona had to say than listen to Roy's lies and bullshit. Tammy told Mona about her conversation at the store and Mona shook her head and told Tammy, "we tried to tell you how he was." "Yo own moma tried to tell you but you wouldn't listen to nobody so we left it alone and let you deal with your own problems."

Tammy was crying so he voice was shakey when she replied to Mona and said "but I love him Mona and I thought he loved me too." Mona said, "it's okay to love someone but it's not okay to keep letting them make a fool out yo ass." Mona told Tammy "it's not shocking to her that Roy got another bitch pregnant, because she had been hearing for months he had different bitches pregnant." Tammy asked Mona "why you never told me?" Mona said "out of all the shit you have already heard was it gone make a fucking difference." "Leslie just told you he had the same bitch that just confronted you, in your car and the bitch done told yo ass she be driving yo shit too." "You sitting up here crying to me instead of going home telling that nigga he needs to get the fuck out yo house." "Yo own fucking son done told you shit." "How much do you have to go through before you wake the fuck up Tammy?" Mona asked her". Tammy looked at Mona and said, "yeah you right." "I'm just gone go home and tell him he has to go." "I can't deal with his shit no mo." While the kids were at school, Tammy decided to go home and tell Roy he had to leave her house. When she pulled up at home she took a deep breath before she walked in the house. Roy was already dressed and ready to leave in her car, Tammy stopped him in his tracks and said, "NO!" "You can't drive my car anymore and you need to get the lil shit you got in my house and leave." Roy turned and looked at Tammy and said "so u putting me out yo shit?" Tammy replied "yup you got to go".

He replied "I'm not tripping Bitch I got plenty places to go!" "I was only here cuz I was using you for your car!" "Why do you think I barely came to this motherfucker!" Tammy replied "well I won't have to worry about you using me for my car anymore because you won't have it." Roy replied "so fucking what!" "I use to have my bitches all in yo shit anyways!" "I even had bitches driving yo shit!" "The bitch at the store wasn't lying either that is my baby she carrying I been fucking with her the whole time I been fucking with you!" "While you thought you was telling her sum shit she already knew I was using yo ass!" "BITCH"! "I never gave a fuck about you!" Tammy got pissed and took a swing at Roy, but he moved his head and leaned toward Tammy and smacked the fuck out of her. He told Tammy "BITCH"! "I wish you would put yo fucking hands on me!" Tammy charged at Roy and he pushed her to the floor. She got up and walked toward him and caught him off guard and hit him in his face. Roy punched Tammy in her nose and made her nose start bleeding.

Tammy swung at him again then Roy punched her in her eye, Tammy fell to the floor again. Her adrenaline was rushing so she felt like she could stand up to him. She got up and charged at him again, he grabbed her by her neck choking her so hard she passed out on the floor. Roy didn't know if she was breathing or not he just grabbed his shit and hurried up and left. Roy was gone leave in Tammy's car but he didn't know if she was dead or not so he left walking and caught the bus so he would have an alibi just in case Tammy was dead. Roy was nervous as hell so he went to his girl crib and told her what had happened and told her if the police come looking for him he gone say he was with her and he wanted her to agree with it. She was down for whatever when it came to Roy that's why he always called her his down ass bitch. Tammy was late picking up the kids the school kept calling her and didn't get an answer.

They were going to call child protective services but they called Tammy's mother instead. While Tammy's mom was on her way to pick up the kids she called Leslie and Mona and asked if they would go to Tammy's house and check on her. Mona had a spare key to get in Tammy's house for emergency purposes. When Mona and Leslie arrived at Tammy's house they saw her car outside, they knocked on the door but didn't get an answer. Mona used her key to open the door and they found Tammy on the living room floor passed out. They could tell she was breathing but they knew something happened because Tammy's face was covered in blood. Leslie went and got some ammonia and put it under Tammy's nose to wake her up and when Tammy came to. She could barely remember anything at that moment. Leslie called Tammy's mom and told her they were on their way to take Tammy to the hospital, her mom yelled through the phone asking for what. Leslie said, "when we got here we didn't get an answer." "Mona used her key to let us in and we found Tammy on the floor beaten up and passed out."

Her mom told Leslie "that bastard did it and I know he did." Leslie said, I'm not sure who done what because Tammy could barely remember what happened to her." Mona knew Roy did it also because Tammy told her she was going home to put Roy out her house. When they arrived at the hospital the nurses was questioning Tammy asking her if she knew who did that to her, Tammy kept saying she couldn't remember. When her mom made it to the hospital and they questioned Tammy again her mother knew she was faking like she couldn't remember to cover up for Roy's punk ass. When the detective came into the emergency room to talk to Tammy, her mother told the detective that Tammy knew who jumped on her and she was covering up for his ass. Her mother told the detectives yall better find his bitch ass before I do. Cuz I don't play about no motherfucker putting his hands on my fucking child. The detective told Tammy's mom to let them handle it and don't end up in jail over some nonsense.

She looked at the detective and said, "do you see my daughters face?" "Do you honestly think I give a fuck about going to jail?" "HELL FUCK NO! The detective replied "everything gone be okay but I need to take this report from your daughter." "If she don't give him up then it's nothing we can do." He asked her mom did she see him put his hands on Tammy. She looked at the detective and said "that is the most stupid shit I have ever been asked." "If I saw him put his hands on my daughter!" "Don't you think if I saw it he would be in here fighting for his life instead of my daughter in here with a fucked up ass face!" The detective knew he wasn't going to get anywhere talking to Tammy's mom. Tammy knew she had to say something or her mom would try and take her kids from her. She threatened to take them if Tammy ever put them in harms ways. Although they wasn't at the house when the fight took place, her mom and friends felt like she was covering for a nigga that disrespected her already and now he done whooped her ass.

They felt like if he did something in front of the kids or to the kids Tammy would cover that up too. Tammy told the detectives what led up to the fight and the last thing she remembered was him punching her in her eye. She then woke up with her friends in front of her asking her what happened to her. The detective asked her if she knew who did that to her and Tammy replied "my boyfriend Roy." They asked Tammy if she knew where Roy could be located and she told them she didn't. Her mom thought she was lying again but Tammy really didn't know because Roy never took her around the people he hung around. She told the detective Roy was probably with his pregnant girlfriend but she didn't know where she lived. Her mom looked over at her and said "what do you mean his pregnant girlfriend?" "You been with him for the last four years and he got a pregnant girlfriend?" Her mom shook her head and said, "We tried to tell you how that nigga was but you ain't want to listen and now he got you out here looking like a damn fool!"

Tammy just put her head down and said "not now ma." "Can we talk about this later?" Tammy's mom asked her "What is it to talk about?" "We tried to tell you and your dumb ass ain't listen so what do we need to talk about?" Tammy just shook her head and kept quiet she knew she couldn't stand a chance arguing back and forth with her mom. The detective wrote up a report and told Tammy she could pick up her police report in two to three business days. Tammy had to go for X-Rays and she found out her nose had been broken and she may have to have surgery on her eye because of the damages he caused to her eye when he punched her. Tammy was sitting on the bed thinking to herself. She couldn't believe Roy would treat her that way after all she had done for him. She knew she couldn't take him back after all the pain and suffering he caused her; she couldn't go back to work because he face was messed up so bad. She didn't want to take the kids to school because she didn't want the teachers asking her what happened and she didn't want the other students picking in the kids because of how she looked. She asked her mom if she would take the kids home with her and take them to school for her.

Her mom told her that she needed to come back home with her also until she heals up. Tammy wasn't gone be able to afford her bills because she didn't have enough sick time left on her job. She was gone be off work about four months and she knew she wasn't gone be able to handle keeping a house. She had to take an FMLA at her job to secure her job and position. The landlord wasn't going to let her break her lease but when his wife found out what happened to Tammy they felt bad for her and decided to let her break the lease so she could go home with her mom. While Tammy was at her mom's house healing after her surgery the police had picked up Roy for domestic battery. He tried to convince the police he wasn't there but Tammy put him there and pointed him as the person who battered her. Even with his girlfriend/new baby mom trying to lie for him it still didn't work in his favor. Roy has a history of beating on women so they knew he was lying. He had never been charged for it. Roy was calling Tammy from jail, trying convince her that he really loved her and asked her if she would drop the charges against him.

Tammy fell for his bullshit and tried to drop the charges behind her mother's back but the state picked up the charges and preceded with their case against Roy. When Roy realized Tammy couldn't drop the charges against him he got pissed and started calling her threatening her life telling her he was gone have some bitches whoop her ass. Tammy knew Roy was lying when he said he really loved her but she wanted to prove everyone wrong about Roy but it didn't work. Leslie asked Tammy what made her love Roy so much after knowing he wasn't shit, and Tammy said "I just like the way he has sex with me." "He gives me a feeling like I never had before." "He knows how to touch me in all the right places and makes me feel so good on the inside." Leslie said "but Tammy you can get sum dick from anywhere." Tammy replied "yeah I know and I have but it's just something about him I can't explain." Leslie shook her head at Tammy and asked "so that nigga had you dick whipped that bad you was gone be stupid for him?" Once again Tammy couldn't say shit. She didn't tell no one how Roy was threatening her from jail, she kept that a secret.

Roy sent bitches to Tammy's old house looking for her to whoop her ass but Tammy had moved and Roy didn't know til the girls told him someone answered the door and said they had just moved there. Roy didn't know where Tammy was staying and her mom's house was the last place he would look because of their previous relationship. He knew her mom barely talked to her. Roy went to court and pleaded not guilty he was sticking to his story that he wasn't there. His baby mom Shania whom previous had words with Tammy over Roy, was going along with that lie until Roy went to court and another bitch showed up for him claiming she was his woman and she had just had a baby 3 months ago by him. When Shania saw the baby and saw that the baby had Roy's last name she went and talked to the prosecutors that was trying Roy for his case that she previous lied about Roy being with her at her house the entire time and that he admitted to her that he jumped on Tammy. The prosecutor asked Shania what made her lie for him if she knew he jumped on Tammy, she responded and said "because she loved him and he is the father of her unborn child". The prosecutor asked Shania what made her recant her story. She replied "because she found out he was treating her the same way he treated Tammy he just didn't put his hands on me". I refuse to allow that to happen." Shania started getting threatening calls from Roy as well after she had spoken to the prosecutors.

Roy felt like she betrayed him and he didn't like no one snitching and being disloyal to him. He expected more out of Shania than he did Tammy because he did have a lil more love for Shania than he did Tammy. Roy was sentenced to 2 years in jail for the battery on Tammy. He stopped calling Shania harassing her but he would still call Tammy asking for her to put money in his books. Tammy refused to put money on his books and she got her number changed. He never called Shania and asked her for shit, she gave birth to his baby while he was locked up. Roy was sitting in jail doing time with barely any money and all the bitches he was messing around with when he was out weren't there for him. He didn't have no one else in his corner. His family didn't fuck with him too much. Roy did his time and was able to get out 6 months early. Neither Shania nor Tammy knew Roy had got out of jail. On night Roy was at his mom house drinking and thinking about a lot of shit that was causing him to get pissed more and more. He decided to pop up at Shania's house he said he wanted to see his baby. Shania knew Roy was drunk because he was reeking of liquor.

All of a Sudden Roy just snapped out and grabbed the 2 by 4 she kept on her door and beat her to death with it. Shania didn't see that coming she thought Roy was coming to see the baby and try to work things out with her. But she lost her life instead. Roy left the house and leaving Shania's body in the house with their 2-month-old baby alone and left and went back to his mom's house. Neighbors kept hearing the baby crying nonstop and they called the police to have them check on the house. When the police arrived and didn't get an answer hey forced their way into the home and found Shania laying their beat to death with her 2 month old baby lying on the couch crying, hungry and dehydrated. The police took the baby to the hospital and got her checked out and waited to contact the next of kin so someone could get the baby if not they was gone turn her over to CPS.

When Tammy learned of Shania's murder she instantly thought of Roy, she was contacted about his early release so she knew he was out. There was no evidence putting Roy on the scene besides his mom never saw him leave the house so she was able to provide an alibi for him. When the authorities learned that Shania helped send him to jail and he was the father of her daughter. His mother never saw him because he went out his room window and when he came back home afterwards he went and set in the living room and watched TV with his mom. She knew he was drinking so she didn't want him to go out and get into trouble. Roy hadn't been the same since he got out of jail. He would have nightmares of him having to fuck around with fags in jail so they would take care him while he was in there. Although he wasn't the one getting fucked he was the one fucking them.

Roy use to fuck with CO's in jail whatever he could do to get by and when one of the CO's caught him fucking a fag she was pissed and started telling the other CO's he was a faggot. One of Roy's boys from the hood found out Roy was fucking around with fags in jail and he didn't want to be around him. He told Roy he lost respect for him cuz all he had was two years and he was fucking with fags when its CO's throwing the pussy at niggas. Roy had knew once everybody found out about him his reputation wasn't gone be shit no mo and he blamed Shania more than Tammy. None of his so-called boys respected him no mo. Although he was never charged with Shania's murder he wasn't shit to nobody in the hood anymore. He couldn't go on the block without niggas talking about him. One day he ran into Tammy and convinced her he was a changed man, Tammy listened to everything he was telling her and it sounded so convincing to her dumb ass she decided to give Roy another chance.

She hid the fact that she was messing back around with Roy from her mom and friends, Roy still lived at his mom's house and Tammy still lived with her mom. Tammy would go and get hotel rooms so she could still fuck around with Roy. Until she ended up pregnant by Roy and she had to reveal to her mom who she was pregnant by. She tried to hide it as long as she could til Mona saw her and Roy in the car together and she knew right then and there Tammy was back fucking with him and that's who knocked her up. During Tammy's pregnancy she started hearing all the rumors about Roy messing with other dudes while he was in jail, but she was scared to ask him. She was hearing it so much she eventually had to ask him and when she did he told her the truth that he was and the reason why.

Tammy felt so disgusted and nasty after hearing Roy tell her the truth. She didn't want her baby anymore and she didn't want to be with Roy anymore either. Roy wasn't trying to let Tammy go, Tammy wanted Roy to herself and now she had him, because didn't nobody else want his ass. Tammy was so embarrassed being with him and when her mom found out everything she was so pissed at Tammy, she put her out and went for custody of the kids. Tammy didn't fight her mom in court she turned over her rights to her mom. Tammy didn't have anywhere to go because Leslie nor Mona would let her live with them so she ended up having to go live with Roy at his mom's house. She tried to ignore all the rumors the best she could eventually she gotten used to it and dealt with it. Roy ended getting a job at a fast food restaurant so he could give his mom money for letting Tammy stay there and Tammy kept going to work so she would be able to provide for her new baby when it arrived. Tammy's mother would only allow her supervised visits with her other children.

Over a period of time the rumors died down. Roy and Tammy stayed together and raised their new son together. Roy changed a lot he was acting like a real boyfriend to Tammy and he was a great father to their son. Tammy would ask Roy about seeing his other children but he would tell her their moms still wouldn't let him see them. The daughter he had by Shania he never wanted to see her because he didn't want to relive the night he killed her mom in front on her and left her on the couch to die of starvation to cover up what he had done. When Tammy would ask him if he knew about what's was going on with Shania's case he would tell her he didn't know anything and he didn't want to talk about it. The way Roy changed his life around Tammy started believing that maybe Roy didn't have anything to do with her murder. In a way Tammy felt like she got what she deserved and somebody killed her for talking too damn much. It was one thing that Tammy was lying down with a man who has previous slept with other men, but she was also lying next to a murderer and didn't have a clue. Shania's case went cold and Roy was never charged with her murder. Roy and Tammy ended up getting married and moving out of town together. Six months into their new life together and their marriage Roy was killed in a car accident by a drunk driver.

Chapter 13

Two years has passed since Desmond had been locked up in D.O.C. He has grown into a full grown twenty one year old man. He got locked up at seventeen right before he turned eighteen. He hasn't seen his family or Krystal in two whole years. He talked to his mom on the phone regularly but he hasn't spoken to Krystal too much on the phone. He was happy to get a visit from his mom, aunt and granny. When he walked into the visitation room they couldn't believe how much he has grown into a man. He has facial hair and his body looked stunning. He sat next to his granny the entire time she wanted to hold him the entire time but you only allowed to hug before the visit and after the visit. Desmond asked his mom why she hasn't sent him any pictures of everybody lately. Her response was she had been working so much trying to find them a new house to move into so she could get away from the old one. Desmond thought that was a great idea because he didn't want to go back there anyways.

He gave his moms Roy information and asked if she could go by the house to see he was there because he was locked up with him and they were real cool. He started writing him but he hadn't responded. He knew he was getting the letters because they never came back to him. Roy kept his word and contacted Desmond now Desmond couldn't understand why he just stopped fucking with him all of a sudden. Talonda promised

Desmond she would go by there and deliver the message to him. They all talked and laughed to keep Desmond's spirits lifted. Talonda felt good that Desmond was okay and he wasn't getting picked on. After the visitation was over Desmond decided to give Krystal a call. He wanted to see where her mind was at after not talking to her for so long. Krystal was still happy to hear from him. She was doing real well after graduating from high school she signed up for college and was still working. Before Desmond could say anything Krystal told him how much she missed him and how she still wanted to be with him. It fucked him up that she was still feeling that way after he was dissing her.

He thought it would make her move on with her life but it didn't. She told Desmond that she was in college so she can get a career that the both of them could benefit from. Desmond wasn't used to hearing shit like that. She had goals she was tryna accomplish and he knew he wanted to do something different with his life once he got out. Desmond knew Krystal was the one for him, but he didn't think he was the one for her. He had a felony hanging over his head that would be there for the rest of his life. Krystal was the type of chick that needed a dude that was doing well also. Krystal whole thing was Desmond could change and she was one help him along the way. She was willing to stick by him and do that. Desmond had never asked Krystal this before but he asked her if she had been fucking anybody. Krystal response was "NO"! I'm still a virgin". Desmond didn't believe her. She told him I will still be a virgin when you get out. If you don't believe me we can go to the doctor together. Desmond just laughed and said, "I'm sorry for asking you that question it was just something I thought about." Krystal knew he would eventually ask her questions like that.

She was okay with it though because she knew she hadn't been doing nothing. She asked him if she could send him some pictures of her and he was trying to make it obvious but he wanted to see some new pics of her bad as hell. Krystal decided to do something even better because she wanted to see him as well. She decided to take off work and take that five hour drive by herself to see the nigga she wanted all to herself in person. The only person knew she was going was Talonda because she was her manger. Talonda wanted to go with her so bad, but she knew Krystal wanted to talk to him all by herself that day. Talonda never told Desmond she was coming she wanted it to be a surprise to him. Desmond wanted to see LOC in person but he couldn't it was so much shit he wanted to talk to him about but he couldn't because they recorded the phone conversations and monitored the mail heavy where he was at.

LOC just made sure Desmond books was straight and stayed out the spotlight. He wasn't tryna give them peoples no reason to fuck with him about shit. Desmond hadn't talked to Dead Eye since he saw him at the funeral. He did put a couple dollars on his books and that was it. Dead Eye wasn't never around when Desmond was out so he was counting on him to be there for him while he's locked up. Desmond felt like LOC was only still around because he was fucking with his auntie. LOC was a stand up nigga though. If he wasn't gone fuck with you he would let it be known. Desmond just felt like everybody else turned on him he was just waiting for the day LOC did it too. Desmond had his moments where he felt like his real peeps was there for him and then he had moments when he felt like everybody was against him. He had been betrayed so much his trust issues was all fucked up.

Desmond called his mom to talk to her, he did that often when he would have mixed feelings about different stuff. Talonda always prayed for her son and made him feel better. Desmond loved his mom no matter how much she fucked up her life in the past. Talonda told Desmond she went by the address he had given her for his friend but the lady that answered the door said no one lived there by that name. Talonda told the lady she was coming over to check on her son's friend because he had been writing him but he hadn't responded. The lady said she hasn't received any mail from no one other than the people who lived there. Desmond told his mom fuck it. Roy knows where he is and if he wanted to holla at him, he would get at him. Talonda asked Desmond what he does in his spare time. He told his mom he has a lil job working in the kitchen and he still write his music and work out that's pretty much all he can do. While he waits to get in the GED classes. So far Desmond was cool. He hollered at a few niggas here and there but not too much. He mainly wanted to focus on what he needed to do to get out of there. He noticed there was a lot of gang activity in jail. More in jail that on the streets. He never wanted to be in a gang or considered himself to be in one and he wasn't about to start now.

When you go to jail for murder people look at you like you are crazy or some shit. Desmond heard all types of stories behind his case, but no one actually knew the facts. People thought he was crazy because he killed his own brother. He let them think whatever they wanted he never discussed his case to one in jail. He didn't want nobody in none of his business. He liked the fact that he didn't have a Bunkie when he first got in there but people was coming in everyday and leaving every day. All he thought about was how he could control his composer if he was housed with a child molester or a rapist. That is what bothered him the most. He would rather be locked up with anybody but one of them. He could even tolerate a fag, as long as they knew he wasn't about that gay shit he was cool with it. He started writing Krystal more and communicating with her like he did when he first caught his case. She was giving him life he was giving her life. They was keeping each other lifted. Krystal was living on the dorm while she was in school. She wanted to be done with school by the time Desmond was released from prison so they could get their own place when he got home. Krystal was going to school for business management. She wanted to own her own business one day.

Desmond liked the fact that she was trying to do something with herself she was motivating him, and she didn't even know it. In the meantime Desmond started studying different stuff so he could prepare himself for the GED classes when it was time for him to take them. He wanted to pass on the first try. Once you flunk you have to wait to do it over. He was tryna knock as much time off his sentence as he could. While he was laying across bunk reading a book. He saw the guard bringing somebody to his room. He didn't want no Bunkie but it wasn't his call. When the dude came in he saw it was old boy Man Man that was locked up with him in juvenile. He was a lil excited to see somebody he actually chopped it up with before. Just because he knew Man Man from juvenile he didn't want to be close with him like that either. He only knew him from being locked up, he ain't know him outside of jail. He kept everything copasetic with him though. Man Man told him about Roy getting killed and that kind of crushed him a lil bit.

He and Roy was closer than him and Man Man was. That fucked him all the way up hearing that. That explains why Roy never responded to any of his letters. Desmond asked Man Man did he get up with Roy in the outside and he told Desmond he was hearing rumors about Roy fucking with niggas and he wasn't about that fag shit. He felt bad he was killed in a car accident but once he started liking niggas he ain't really have no holla for him. Desmond asked Man Man how did he find out Roy was killed in a car accident. He told him when he was in the county and a couple of dudes knew Roy that's how he found out he was on dat fag shit. One of the dudes said he heard he moved out of town with that broad he was with and ended up getting hit by a drunk driver. All Desmond could do was shake his head in disbelief. He kind of hated he was sharing a cell with a nigga from around his surrounding areas because he didn't want to hear all the negative shit that was going on out I the streets. Desmond wanted to see how Man Man was gone carry himself in jail, he didn't want him to think that he was gone be in no bullshit with him. Man Man was wild ass fuck when he was a juvie. Desmond knew ain't shit changed since that nigga got a lil older. He probably worse than he was as a juvie. He been in and out of jail damn near his entire life.

He gotta do five years in the joint for selling dope to an informant. Man Man knew a lot of the motherfuckers that was locked up with them. Desmond ain't care who he knew he just wanted to focus on his own shit. Man Man came in with no money on his books because they took all his money from him when he was arrested. His mom never came to see him in juvenile, so Desmond knew she wasn't gone put no money on his books. Desmond thought Man Man moma just didn't care about him. She was up in age when she had Man Man, she was 42 when she gave birth to him. She did he best to keep him on the right path, but he decided to go left with his life. Desmond wasn't gone let him go without while he was in there. If he ate then Man Man was gone eat too. That's the type of person Desmond was. He would give his last to anybody in need, because he knew what it was like not to have shit. The only thing Desmond didn't like was that Man Man would be gossiping with them other niggas like a lil bitch. Every time sum shit jumped off he was always in the middle of the shit. Desmond tried to tell him to just be cool and get him a lil job so he can do his time and go to the crib. Man Man was a hot head nigga though, you couldn't tell him shit.

He was gone do what he wanted to do anyways. He had a few chicks he could call while he was locked up, but they would never come and see him or put money on his books. Desmond realized why they didn't when he heard how he be talking to them on the phone. Every time he talked to one of them he was calling them bitches and hoes. Desmond couldn't see himself talking to Krystal the way Man Man was talking to his broads. Desmond received his letter that he could start his GED classes earlier than what he thought. He was gone be able to start the following week coming up. He was excited about that. He called to tell his mom abut she didn't answer the phone. He knew she was probably at work, or she would have answered. He called his granny to tell her the good news. He barely called her because he didn't want her to think the worse. He only wanted to talk to her when he had good news to tell. She was so happy to hear from Desmond she couldn't wait for him to get home. They refrained from bringing up DJ's name to him while he was in there, because they knew he already took it hard and they wanted his mind to be at ease.

Desmond was fairly quiet but when he got pissed off he became a different person. Desmond put his music off for a while to focus on his studies for the GED. He really wanted to get that, it would take six month off his time. He got nine months taken off for completing three programs. He can't take anymore programs all he could do was take the GED and finish whatever time he had left to do. Desmond did a total of three years in jail already and he was going on his fourth year. He kept himself so busy so he won't be focusing on the time that has already passed. He tried talking Man Man into getting in the programs to get some time lifted off his sentence but he wasn't tryna hear all that shit Desmond was talking about. Desmond just let him do him and he didn't worry about it nomo. He saw Man Man wasn't tryna do right in jail so he knew he had to be reckless as hell outta jail. He was cursing out the guards and sent to lock down. He was just constantly fucking up. The more he fucked up the more they was tryna add time onto him. Desmond started think that nigga never wanted to get out of jail by the way he was acting. Man Man was tryna get him a lil hustle going on in jail with all the shit Desmond helped him get. Desmond didn't know anything about making money in jail. He just wanted to be neutral as possible so he could go to the crib.

Desmond knew he had to distant himself before he ended up in all kinds of shit. While they were in chow Man Man got into it with two dudes over sum tobacco. Desmond felt like he was gone have to help him if they started scrapping because they was cool. They guards came over and diffused the situation and Desmond was relieved. Desmond starting seeing how easy it was to get involved in sum shit in jail. The entire time he was there he never had any problems. Desmond tried talking to Man Man but he so damn stupid he won't listen to shit nobody tells him. Desmond told Man Man he ain't tryna end up in no bullshit. He wants to do his time and go to the crib. Man Man response was "I don't give no fuck!" "I didn't tell you to get in my shit anyways nigga!" "I been holding my own down!" Fuck You!" Desmond looked at Man Man and shook his head. He couldn't believe the nigga he looked out for all that time was talking to him crazy. Desmond just kept shaking his head at Man Man. Desmond was far from scared of him, he just didn't want to go there with dude, because he thought they were cool. Desmond knew once Man Man food and hygiene was gone that was it.

He wasn't buying him shit else. He was on the urge of risking his time cuts to help that nigga and he played him like that. The entire time they were locked down Desmond didn't utter one word to Man Man and he didn't utter one word to Desmond. The next day while they was in Chow Desmond noticed that when he went to sit at the table sum cats started acting funny with him and not tryna let him sit down. Desmond didn't trip; he just went to another table. When he sat down he noticed Man Man was giggling because they would let Desmond sit at the table. Desmond kept his cool, he tried to avoid every situation possible. Desmond knew at that very moment he couldn't trust Man Man no longer. Desmond vowed to never take another life but if he had to he would. If Roy was in there with them Man Man wouldn't be fucking with Desmond, because he knew they were cool.

Man Man didn't fuck with Roy too tuff, because he was scared of him. Desmond sat and observed Man Man, he knew he wasn't as tuff as he wanted people to think he was. Desmond knew without a shadow of doubt he could kick Man Man ass. He saw how Man Man was when them other dudes confronted him about their tobacco he owed them. He didn't get tuff with them until he saw how Desmond raised up and he knew that if sum shit jumped off, Desmond had his back. He knew that wasn't over because Man Man still owed them and they wasn't going to let it ride. Desmond was waiting for the moment when Man Man got into sum mo shit. When Desmond made his commissary he only bought enough for himself and Man Man was fucked up about it. Desmond knew Man Man didn't have no money, and the lil hustle he had going he couldn't keep up. Man Man need sum of his commissary to keep his hustle going. Man Man started talking bad about Desmond to other inmates. He was telling them how Desmond wacked his own brother. That was a sensitive topic for Desmond and Man Man knew it.

All of a sudden Desmond was getting questioned throughout the jail about killing his brother. One cat came up to Desmond and asked him what made him wack his own brother. Desmond held his composer and responded it was a mistake so I would appreciate if you didn't believe everything you hear. Desmond wasn't tryna be rude about it. He just ain't like discussing it with nobody. Desmond knew only one person could be spreading his business and he knew it was Man Man. Desmond never confronted Man Man he acted as if he didn't give a shit. Man Man didn't like that Desmond wasn't showing no emotion. He wanted to piss Desmond off and do whatever he could to try and get Desmond's ass whooped in jail. Man Man would go and tell other niggas that Desmond said shit about them and had niggas confronting Desmond about sum bullshit that he never done. Desmond had already had in his mind that he would risk his freedom and get sum mo time before he let any of them niggas punk him or whoop his ass.

Desmond never had to play dirty before but he knew that if he sat back too much longer Man Man was gone try and get him into it with as many people as he could. Desmond knew he could've kited out the section, but he would have to explain why. In jail that's a form of dry snitching. He was use to being where he was at and he wasn't about to let Man Man bitch ass fuck dat up for him. Desmond tried to stay level headed but he knew eventually he was gone have to fuck Man Man up. He ain't wanna go there with him, but he was doing bogus shit that Desmond wasn't going for. Desmond knew that it would be him or another nigga in there. Desmond was glad he was able to start his GED classes early, that gave him time out of the section and time away from Man Man shit starting ass.

For once in a very long time Desmond was happy to be doing something right. He gotten nine months knocked off his sentence for taking different classes the prison offered to them. When Desmond would get back to his cell he focused on his homework and studying for his test. Desmond started noticing that some of his noodles and summer sausages would be missing and he knew it was Man Man stealing his shit. He started not to say nothing, but he wasn't about to let Man Man think he could do whatever he wanted to when it came to his shit either. Desmond caught Man Man in chow and confronted him about stealing his food. Man Man called his self-jumping hard with Desmond because he thought he was really a punk. Just because Desmond shot his brother he thought Desmond wasn't shit without a gun. Desmond's adrenaline was on 10 so he was ready for whatever. Man Man called himself jumping toward Desmond and trying to muff him on the low.

As soon as he missed Desmond rocked his ass one time and dropped his bitch ass. A couple inmates came and separated the two before the guards locked everybody down. Desmond just proved to everybody that he wasn't no hoe ass nigga, like Man Man tried to play him as. Man Man was knocked out for about 5 minutes before he was picked up off the floor by the two niggas that broke up the fight. When the guards ran into the chow room, they was questioning other inmates about the incident. They knew Man Man was a part of it because his mouth was leaking after Desmond cracked his ass. They asked Man Man who was the other person involved and he wouldn't tell. Desmond told on his self because he knew if they found it was him it would fuck up all his time cuts and his GED classes. When the Sargeant interviewed both men they told different stories. Man Man told then that Desmond was mad and punched him because he was on some gay shit and he didn't get down with that shit.

Desmond told them that he confronted Man Man about stealing his food and Man Man tried to sucker punch him and he hit him one time and that was the end of the fight. The Sargeant asked Desmond if he had tried to make sexual advances toward Alvin Boston (Man Man). Desmond looked at the Sargent with a pissed off look cleared his throat and said "FUCK NO!" He then apologized for cursing and responded again saying no sir. I am not gay Sarg. I never asked or talked to that man on a level like that. The Sarg told Desmond he will review the tapes and go from there before he see if the both of them or one of them would be charged for the incident. Desmond wasn't tripping because he knew he ain't do shit. In the meantime both guys was sent to the hole until the investigation was over. Desmond was in the hole for four days.

The Sarg and the Warden reviewed he tape and saw that Man Man swung on Desmond first so Man Man was charged with battery. They didn't know what lead to the fighting but they saw Man Man was the initiator. Man Man had to do ninety days in the hole and Desmond was release back into population. He wasn't able to attend his GED class for three days. The instructor was nice enough to let him make up the work he missed. The GED instructor was pretty cool. Her name was Ms. Baker. They thought she would be on bullshit because she was young and pretty. Most of the young broads that work there always walked around with their nose stuck up. Ms. Baker was friendlier than the others besides teaching GED classes she would do prison ministry at the prison also for the inmates. After Desmond was released everyone was asking him what broke out between him and Man Man.

Desmond told them he confronted him about stealing his commissary. Desmond also told them what Man Man had told the Sarg. They was tripping off that bullshit because as long as Desmond been locked up ain't no rumors ever surfaced about him fucking with dudes in the joint. Man Man didn't know he lost a lot of respect from the few that did respect him for that bullshit. Now that Desmond had Man Man out the way he was able to focus on the shit he needed to focus on. For the next three months Desmond focused on studying for his GED. After being in the hole for ninety days Man Man was released back into population. He no longer shared cellies with Desmond nomo.

He was still in the same pod just a different cell. He was moved in the cell with Big Rico. Big Rico was an Illegal Immigrant from Mexico. He was locked for being a part of a Mexican Drug Cartel. He used to help them shipped cocaine from Mexico to the states. Big Rico had been locked up for 15 years already and he still had thirty mo years to go. You can tell he had been down for a while because he had all the luxuries in his cell. He had a TV, Mp3, radio, different shoes to choose from, an entire jail wardrobe, and damn near an entire grocery area. His people on the outside took damn good care of him. He mainly stayed off to himself. He didn't come out to often, he spent a lot of his time drawing cartoon pics for different inmates and making different stuff to store their hygiene in. He was real talented with his hands. He always tried to talk to the younger generation about correcting their lives once they touch down on the outside. At the same time he didn't play with none of them neither. He was a well-respected OG in the joint. He got along with all races. What fucked a lot of people up was he was well-respected by the Arian brothers too. He was showed a lot of love through the system.

Chapter 14

Another year has passed and Desmond passed his GED test. That's another six months taken off his time. Desmond's family was so excited for him. Desmond noticed since Man Man has been bunkies with Big Rico he hasn't been doing a lot of the stupid shit he was doing at first. Big Rico paid off Man Man's debt for him and keeping him grounded. There were rumors going around the joint that Man Man was Big Rico's bitch in jail. Desmond was starting to believe it too, because he did do a drastic change about himself. Man Man was calmer than he has ever been. Big Rico didn't pay the rumors any attention he was there to help out all the youngsta's if he could. He definitely didn't have to fuck no niggas in jail. He was knocking off all the female guards. Fucking boys wasn't his thing. He knew Man Man needed guidance and once Man Man told Big Rico about his lifestyle and how the streets taught him how to survive that was all he knew.

Big Rico knew Man Man would eventually get himself killed in jail if he kept up with the bullshit he was doing. Big Rico told Man Man he would pay his debt off for him but only on one condition. He wanted Man Man to start getting involved in some of the activities the jail offered and get enrolled into sum GED classes so he could get some education. Man Man didn't know much of shit. Big Rico told him that it was cool be have street sense but he needed some book knowledge as well. Big Rico couldn't be there for his own kids so he focused on helping the ones up under him get the credentials they need so they can live a prosperous life outside of jail. He would still fuck a nigga up if he had too though. Just when Desmond thought Man Man got himself together, he ended up getting into so mo shit. He thought just because Big Rico had love thought out the jail and he was his Bunkie niggas wouldn't do shit to him.

Man Man had been under handing Big Rico all along. He had been using the shit Rico was getting him on commissary to make extra money. Rico told him that he would help him out of that one debt but he bet not get his ass into shit else. Sho nuff his dumb ass got into sum shit with the Arian brothers. Everybody in jail knows them not the ones to fuck with. They had been fronting Man Man tobacco and he was supposed to make triple, and every time one of Arians approach Man Man about their money he kept making excuses. Man Man couldn't pull that shit on Big Rico like he had done Desmond. Although the Arians respected Rico they still didn't play about their shit. Meanwhile while Man Man is trying to keep the Arians off his ass. Desmond received sum good news his parole hearing was coming up. He will be going up against the parole board once he completed seven years of his sentence and he didn't have long to go. He didn't want to get to happy because he knows that they can deny your parole just as quick as they can give it to you.

Desmond hated Man Man so much he use to wish it was Man Man he killed instead of his brother. He looked out for Man Man like he was one of his real friends and he stabbed him in the back in a fucked up way. He tried to put a hit on his head by lying on him to other niggas in the joint. Desmond still thinks about how he lied about him making sexual advances toward him. He often thought about paying the Arians off on his own but for them to fuck Man Man up and it would still leave Man Man owing them his own debt. He knew he had to keep it low because niggas in jail talk like bitches. He didn't want nothing to fuck up his parole hearing. He thought long and hard about it, but he let up on it. He decided to just leave it alone. When Rico caught wind that Man Man owed the Arians money after he paid off his debt before he beat Man

Man ass his self. He caught Man Man in the shower and beat the fuck out his ass. Big Rico then told Man Man he wanted all his money back for the previous debt he paid for him too. Now that left Man Man owing the Arians and Big Rico.

No one really trusted Man Man so it would be hard for him to pay the both of them off. When Man Man was questioned about his bruises and black eyes he kept quiet. He knew that Big Rico had a lot of niggas that respected him and if he told on Big Rico it would be a deadly situation and he would definitely be leaving outta there with a nametag on his toe. Man Man knew he couldn't stand a chance so he wrote the warden asking if he could be moved to another jail because he feared his life. The guard he gave the letter too was a guard that Big Rico was linked up with. The guard told Big Rico what Man Man had done. Big Rico played it cool and had Man Man thinking he didn't know anything about it. Big Rico decided he would let the Arians do the job for him. He couldn't afford to get moved because his family moved from their home town to be closer to him and if he gotten into any trouble it was a good chance he would get shipped to another jail. Rico hollered at the Arians and told them when to make their move. He went on with his everyday routine so Man Man wouldn't think shit.

About four days later Man Man was found hanging in his cell by a female guard. The news spreaded through the jail pretty damn quick that, Man Man was found hanging in his cell. Instantly Desmond started to feel bad and wishing it was something he could've done to help him, but he was in too deep. You would've thought he learned his lesson but he didn't. He thought he could gank them niggas in jail like he did them motherfuckers out on the street. He had reached a point when he realized the game was just too cold for his ass. Everybody was trying to figure out who killed Man Man but it wasn't nobody talking. The Arians was pissed because they wanted to have the pleasure of doing him in their selves. Desmond was questioned about his murder because he worked part-time as a janitor in the jail.

No one knew who did it. Two weeks later Desmond went in front of the parole board and was granted his parole. He thought while Man

Man's murder was still under investigation it would hold up his hearing but he was able to go home. While he was getting his things together he overheard Rico telling the guard in the hallway where he could go pick up his payment from when he got off. Desmond knew right then and there Rico paid the guard to kill Man Man for him. He acted as if he didn't hear anything and continued to pack up his belongings and waited for his out date. He called LOC for the first time ever from a nigga's cell phone, that he had in jail and told him he was granted parole and he would be released the following Monday. He didn't want nobody to know he was getting released.

When the day finally came for Desmond to be released from prison. He didn't call his mom or Krystal to tell them he was coming home. After serving seven long years a lot has changed in Desmond's life. At the age of 24 Desmond stood at 5'10" tall. His body was sculptured to perfection. Desmond didn't leave jail like an average nigga that just got released in sweats and a t-shirt. LOC made sure he left the joint on point. He had him a pair of Robbins Jeans with the matching t-shirt and a fresh pair of Jordans. His hair was faded nice and neat. His face was lined so good it made his lips look plush and soft like pillows. He knew he was looking good too. Over the years he did get a lil arrogance about himself, especially when all those female guards was throwing pussy at him.

He never fucked none of them but it was a few he wanted to dick down. He was tempted many times but he knew them bitches was fucking all around the joint. Some of them was married but they was getting fucked by the inmates more than they was by their husbands. They didn't have rubbers in jail and he wasn't about to fuck them bitches raw. A lot of them tough niggas was fucking other niggas. He preferred to beat his on meat. LOC and Tracey had been kicking it off real good. So good to the point LOC told Desmond his aunt was four months pregnant by him. Tracey never mentioned to Desmond that she was pregnant. Desmond was happy for the both of them. Desmond was so eager to get home to see his family. His mom had moved to the other side of town because she had so many bad memories in her old house.

She wanted a fresh start for her and the kids. After five long hours of driving home. Desmond and LOC pulled up at Desmond mom's house. Desmond saw his younger brother and sisters outside playing and riding their bikes LOC and Tracy bought them. The younger kids didn't really remember Desmond. He looked so different to them. He had no facial hair when he first left now he has a full beard and mustache. As he approached the door to walk in the house Shelly saw him and ran toward the door giving him the biggest hug she could give him with tears flowing down her face. She hadn't seen him in years. Their mom was at work she still didn't know Desmond was home and he didn't want them to tell her.

Shelly called Krystal over to the house so Desmond could surprise her. LOC knew once Desmond saw Krystal he knew he was gone want sum pussy from her lil thick ass. He asked Desmond if was gone chill at the crib or did he want to get a room for him and his girl for the night. Desmond wanted to go to the room but he wanted to see his mom and grandparents first. Desmond hadn't had no pussy since him and DJ went to the hotel the night of DJ's birthday. He was kid then and he pleased a grown experienced stripper real good. So he knew once he got ahold of Krystal's ass he was gone tear her lil tight virgin pussy up. Jacking off wasn't the same feeling as the inside of that warm wet womb. Krystal was a twenty three year old virgin. She was saving herself for Desmond and Desmond only. When Krystal arrived at Talonda's house she wasn't expecting to see Desmond. When she saw him she was stunned, her bottom lip started to shake as she was trying so hard to hold back her tears. She waited so long for that day to come and it felt like she was waiting forever.

She hugged Desmond so tight and didn't want to let him go. Desmond never been the disrespectful type but he couldn't resist. He grabbed and palmed her big ol' round ass and caressed it with both hands. He waited seven long years to grab that ass. Krystal didn't give him a chance to kiss her, she grabbed his face with both hands and preceded to twirl her tongue up against his tongue. The more she kissed and sucked his tongue the more her panties moistened. She use to stimulate herself with different sex toys she had bought while thinking and waiting for him. She had to break away from Desmond and cool herself off. It felt good while she was stimulating herself so she knew if would feel even better bumping pelvises with the one she love. She had to excuse herself and go to the bathroom to wipe herself, her pussy was soaking wet after that kiss. Krystal couldn't wait til later she was ready to give Desmond all of her. While she was cleaning herself off, Desmond came to the bathroom door to make sure she was good. She was far from good she had gotten pissed all of a sudden. He period was about to start. She thought she had calculated her dates and her period wasn't supposed to come for another week. The wet tingling feeling she was getting was her period not her cummin on herself or her body secretions.

She couldn't believe she waited all that time for the day to come to finally fuck her man and her fucking period starts. Krytal refused to wait any longer. She was gone still fuck her man. She googled different ways on how to stop your period. If she had to fuck on her period she was gone have do that too. She didn't want Desmond to know because she didn't want him to refuse. Desmond had a lil mo experience than Krystal. She self-taught herself how to please him. She would take the dildo she bought and licked, slob and slurped all over it t was Desmond. She would stroke her clit with her middle finger giving it a lil stimulation so she could cum. Krystal couldn't wait for Talonda to get off work. In the meantime she found out from the internet that if you take Ibuprofen it would stop your period, so while on the way taking Desmond to see his grandparents she stopped at the gas station to buy a few packs of Ibuprofen and some bottle water.

While they were riding through his old hood he wanted to see Dead Eye since he hadn't heard from him in a while. When they arrived at Moma Tanya's house she couldn't do nothing but break down with tears of joy. As she saw her handsome grandson transition into a grown man walk through her door. Tracey was at moma Tanya's house when Desmond arrived. Tracey wobbled over to her nephew and gave him a welcome home hug. Moma Tanya starred at Desmond and saying to herself how much he look likes his older brother DJ. He looked so much like DJ that moma Tanya was starting to think that Mr. B was probably his father too. She hurried and blocked those delusional thoughts from her mind very quickly. She still didn't want to believe that scenario, but she knew her daughter wouldn't lie about nothing like that. She turned her focus to her grandson who was finally home after seven years.

Desmond hugged and kissed his grandfather on his forehead and told him he missed and loved him. His grandfather had Alzheimer's so he didn't remember Desmond at all. Talonda had to close so after visiting his grandparents and aunt he went to surprise his mom at her job. When she saw Desmond walk into her store she tried to hold her composer because she was at work. She gave her son the biggest hug a mother could give their child. She couldn't prevent her tears from flowing down her face either. She introduced Desmond to her co-workers. Krystal wasn't too fond of that. She saw how the new bitch Tiff kept starring at her man. Krystal never trusted Tiff, girls always coming up to the job tryna whoop her ass over their nigga. Krystal even heard that Tiff fucked her own sisters dude, so she really ain't wont her around her nigga. Desmond told his mom he would be there in the morning to take her to breakfast but he was gone go and chill with Krystal for the night.

While Desmond was out seeing his mom LOC picked up Tracey and they went to rent Desmond a room for the night. Tracey couldn't believe her lil nephew was a grown man but she wanted his first night home to be special. She decorated the room with rose petals, warming oils, whipped cream and chocolate covered strawberries. LOC tried to explain to her that Desmond wasn't gone be into all that shit and it would be a waste of money. She insisted on doing it and making it extra special for him. Afterwards she understood LOC's point she knew Desmond wouldn't be thrilled by none of that shit Krystal still hadn't told Desmond her period came down, she wanted too because she had been honest with him about everything else. In the back of her mind she felt like if she didn't fuck him he would go and get it elsewhere.

She was not about to let that happen. He had some pure fresh meat and she wanted it. When they arrived at the room Krystal fell in love with everything Tracey did. She thought it was all Desmond's idea and he was just as surprised as she was. He actually liked it. He was thinking about all kinds of freaky shit when he saw that whipped cream. Krystal went to take a shower and she noticed her period didn't come all the way down. She figured the Ibuprofen trick worked. While she was in the shower Desmond took off his clothes and joined her. He took the body wash and poured it on her back and rubbed the soap all over her back with his hands. He pulled her ponytail holder out her head so her hair could drape long pass her shoulders as she held her head under the water. Desmond watched as the water ran done her body. He groped her titties with his hands as he began to stimulate her nipples with his tongue. He kissed her all over her body giving her a tingling sensation.

He squatted down and put her legs over his shoulders as he lifted her into the air with her legs still over his shoulders he began to lick and taste her body fluids giving her an erotic sensation. He could feel her strength lifting away from her body as he continued to please her with his tongue. He used the strength from his strong arms and shoulders as he lifted her higher into the air and licked her from back to front. As her body began to quiver he licked the juices from her body as she squirted them out. He lowered her to his waste and slid his dick into her pussy and took slow long strokes into the walls of her pussy. She tightened up her walls as he stroked her long and hard. She rubbed his muscle tone body gently as she kissed him on his neck. As the both of them continued to moan from the feeling of each other's sexual organs. They kissed and sucked on one another. He lowered her to her feet and she squatted and grabbed his nine inches and began to tease the tip of his dick with her tongue.

She licked it up and down and sucked the tip of him until he stiffened as hard as he could. Then she deep throated his meat as she looked at up him while she gagged. The more she saw his eyes roll into the back of his head she continued to suck him until his knees weakened. He wasn't ready to nutt so he pulled out her mouth and sucked on her titties some more. He bent her over and watched the water run through her hair as he fucked and slapped her on her ass. He always wanted to know what it felt like to kiss a woman while bustin inside her at the same time. So he fucked her from the back as the crawled out the tub to the bathroom floor. She turned over into the missionary position and he slid back into her. He loved listening to the wet sound her pussy was making every time he dug deeper into her womb. His body stiffened as he was about to nutt. He kissed and tickled her with his tongue as he released his body fluids into her and making her cum at the same time.

Afterwards all Desmond could do was lay on her for a few. He had gotten a lil light headed after that. The both of them took a shower and went to bed. They took each other's energy after that nutt. They never got the chance to use the condiments Tracey placed in the room for them. The next day Desmond took his mom and siblings to breakfast. Krystal had to work although she didn't want to go. Talonda was telling Desmond how her co-worker Tiff kept asking her questions about him. Talonda really liked Krystal and that's who she wanted Desmond to be with. She didn't want Desmond to mention to Krystal that Tiff been asking about him because she knows how Krystal feels about her. After breakfast they all went back to the house so Desmond could catch up on everything he had missed out on.

He saw his mom had a new truck so he was ready to get his L's so he could be whipping her shit. Talonda thought it was a good idea for him to get them also, especially since he had to go and check in with parole often. If she had to work and Krystal had to work he could take his self. He studied the book from time to time in jail, so he asked his mom to take him to take the permit test. He took the test and got his permit on the first try. He couldn't drive unless it was a license driver in the car with him but he was cool with that. Where they're from you only gotta wait ninety days to take the driver's test. LOC let him drive around to make sure he had it down pack. DJ was the one that drove all the time when they were out.

Desmond was tryna get out and make up for lost time and Krystal wanted to be under him every chance she got. She stopped going to school just so she could lay up under him but he wasn't the type of nigga to lay around. He had enough of that shit in jail. Desmond love Krystal but he knew she meant well, he just wasn't use to all they laying up all day and all night shit. It was cool in the beginning but he was ready to live life. He already gave seven years to the state. She was crowding him and making him feel like he was still locked up. She started popping up at his moms crib every day and mentally that's not the type of relationship he wanted. He wanted to feel free. He was still emotionally dealing with the loss of his brother. Although he never brought it up he thought about him every day. He decided to go and get DJ's face tattooed on his back. It made Desmond feel like DJ was still with him every day. When Desmond got his driver's license he didn't even want to tell Krystal because she was gone be expecting to ride with him everywhere he went.

LOC was his only riding buddy but he had his own life with Tracey. He still hadn't seen Dead Eye out anywhere. He didn't want to take the chance and ride by the spot because he was on papers. Desmond would drop his moms off at work and keep her truck. While he was dropping her off Tiff made it her business to come and say something to him. They talked for a minute and exchanged numbers. Tiff didn't waste no time calling Desmond. She invited him over to her house for some drinks. At first he didn't want to go but he thought it was just a friendly thing so he went over and chilled with her for a couple of hours. He took a couple shots of Patron and talked to her for a while. Tiff wasn't really a drinker the Patron was getting the best of her and Desmond was looking sexy as fuck to her. She initiated the situation and Desmond ended up fucking her not thinking that he had a faithful girl at the crib.

Afterwards he realized what he had done and left and went to the crib. He knew Tiff worked with his mom and Krystal. He texted tiff and told her he didn't mean for that to happen and it needs to stay between them. Tiff was okay with it at first but when he wouldn't respond to any of her texts or calls. She started throwing subliminal shots at Krystal. Krystal wasn't catching on to any of it. She thought Tiff was just being the same ol' messy ass Tiff so she ignored her. Desmond stopped responded to Tiff once Krystal told him how she keep saying lil smart shit to her for no reason. A month later Tiff announces at work she was pregnant. The other co-workers were excited for her and was discussing on when they would give her a baby shower. She text Desmond and told him she was pregnant.

His heart jumped out his body. He texted back, and asked her what she was telling him for. She texted back and said, because it's yours. Desmond said, bullshit that ain't my fuckin baby you better text the real daddy. Deep down inside Desmond knew he fucked that bitch without a rubber. He tried to be cool and tell Tiff that he wasn't ready for no kids, but she wasn't tryna hear that. She knew it would eat Krystal up on the inside. Desmond didn't want her to have that baby for shit. He wasn't even ready for no kids. Tiff wasn't goin she was determined to keep her baby. Desmond thought of a million ways to get her to lose that baby. He even wanted to pay a bitch to whoop her ass to keep from her having that baby. He knew jail time wasn't worth it though. He could talk to his mom about everything but that. If it was his baby he was damn sho gone hide it from everybody including his family. Tiff wanted the truth to get out so bad so she decided to tell one of her co-workers.

That bitch couldn't hold water. If she knew anything she was gone tell it and Tiff knew that. Tiff told her co-worker Reesie that she was pregnant by Talonda's son. Reesie didn't believe her at first because Desmond was just too fine to mess with a dusty broad like Tiff. Ressie did just what Tiff wanted her to do she asked Talonda was she happy she was about to be a grandmother. Talonda looked at her sideways and asked "when Krystal get pregnant?" Reesie had a blank look on her face and said "uhmmmmm no" "Not Krystal" but uhmmmmm you ain't hear it from me, Tiff told me she pregnant by your son." Talonda responded "well she's a damn lie, she ain't fucked with my son!" Talonda couldn't wait to get home to talk to Desmond. She texted him and told him to be on time picking her up because they needed to talk. Right then and there Desmond just knew what it was about. He had a gut feeling Tiff was going to tell his mom. He called Tiff and asked her why in the fuck she tell his mom. She swore on bibles she didn't tell his mom. She failed to tell him that she told her co-worker though. Desmond dreaded going to pick up his mom and the time was moving very quickly. When he picked up his mom the first thing she asked him was "Why Desmond?" "Why did you sleep with that girl?" "You knew how Krystal felt about her!" Desmond couldn't respond. He took a deep breath and said, "It just happened all of a sudden."

Desmond hadn't been home six months and fucked up already. Talonda asked him was it a possibility it was his baby. He looked at his mom and said "we was drinking a few shot of Patron and it just happened." Talonda asked, "Why didn't you at least use protection, son?" Once again Desmond didn't have an answer. Talonda was off the next day so she wouldn't see Tiff until the following day. She wanted to humble Tiff real good about her son. Talonda knew Krystal was a damn good girl and she didn't deserve what Desmond done to her. Krystal was at the house when they arrived and Desmond couldn't look at her in the face. He was pissed at his own self. Krystal could tell something was wrong she didn't know what though. Talonda wanted Desmond to keep it on hush until they found out if the baby was really his. By the next day the entire job knew Tiff was pregnant by Talonda's son.

Krystal was heated at work when she found out the news. She started to feel sick to her stomach and had to leave. She felt like that's why Desmond kept telling her he needed some space so he could fuck other bitches. Krystal raced to Talonda's house and questioned Desmond about it but he looked at her in her face and lied. He told her he never fucked Tiff and she was just saying sum shit to piss her off. Talonda started seeing symptoms from Desmond. He would sleep all day and eat up everything in the house. She knew that was his baby. She told him, "You need to tell Krystal the truth so she could move on with her life." Desmond's head was all fucked up. He ain't want no baby by her dusty ass.

He knew he had fucked up too. Time was progressing and Desmond knew he was running out of time and the truth was gone hit the fan. When it was time for Tiff to give birth she tried calling Desmond but he wouldn't answer. He missed the birth of his baby. Talonda went up to the hospital and as soon as she took one look at Tiff's baby boy. She knew it was her grandson. He looked identical to Desmond when he was a baby. Talonda called Desmond up to the hospital because it was time for him to own up to his responsibilities. He came up to the hospital so he could sign the birth certificate. It was nowhere to run it was time for him to be a man and face his responsibilities. He named his first son after his brother DJ. He finally told Krystal the truth. The news hurted her so bad that she got her number changed and moved out of town to go back to school. Desmond didn't have no thoughts of being with Tiff he just wanted to co-parent with her. Krystal has never spoken to Desmond or his family ever again.

The End

Milton Keynes UK
Ingram Content Group UK Ltd.
UKHW020727120923
428521UK00014B/588